D0055868

"Have I ever told you how your beautiful eyes helped ground me? And did you know you have tiny green and gold flecks in them?"

She shook her head, mesmerized by the confession.

"I was panicking about being trapped inside my body, and there you were, confident and gentle. You helped me remember I was still human." His hand gently threaded through her hair.

His face grew blurry as involuntary tingles started behind her lids. She blinked to bring him back into focus.

"I knew when you were here with me I was safe. Someone would fight *for* me—even if it meant fighting *me*. I knew you gave a damn."

Enthralled by his gaze, she swallowed a swell of emotion, and subtly moistened her lips.

Steady hands guided her face to his. Looking her soundly in the eyes, he placed a long, luscious kiss on her lips…

Lynne Marshall has been a registered nurse in a large hospital in California for over twenty years. Currently she is an advice/triage nurse for fifteen internal medicine doctors. She began writing in 2000, and has earned over a dozen contest awards since. She is happily married to a police lieutenant, and has a grown daughter and son. Besides her passion for writing Medical™ Romance stories, she loves travel, reading, and power walks. Lynne's website is www.lynnemarshallweb.com

Recent titles by the same author:

HER L.A. KNIGHT
HER BABY'S SECRET FATHER

IN HIS
ANGEL'S ARMS

BY
LYNNE MARSHALL

MILLS & BOON®
Pure reading pleasure

First published in Great Britain 2007
Large Print edition 2008
Harlequin Mills & Boon Limited,
Eton House, 18-24 Paradise Road,
Richmond, Surrey TW9 1SR

© Lynne Marshall 2007

ISBN: 978 0 263 19928 4

Set in Times Roman 16½ on 19¾ pt.
17-0108-49598

Printed and bound in Great Britain
by Antony Rowe Ltd, Chippenham, Wiltshire

IN HIS
ANGEL'S ARMS

In loving memory of Don Coppinger.
God Bless.

CHAPTER ONE

MALLORY GLENN shuddered at the thought of not being able to breathe.

She used sterile gloves and a flexible catheter to deep-suction the bronchi and lungs of her patient through the tracheostomy. She'd exchanged the inner removable cannula and cleaned the remaining tube in record time, as she'd had to remove the patient from the ventilator to do it. In between, she aerated him with four manual pumps on the ambu-bag.

Once she'd put her patient back on the ventilator to catch his breath, and the strained look in his eyes had subsided, she felt comfortable enough to suction more. He coughed and sputtered, but his airway toiletry had been done to the best of her ability. She expected no less of herself in whatever function she performed at Los Angeles Mercy Hospital.

Mallory smiled and reassuringly patted the patient's shoulder. He returned the look with a nod indicating that all was well.

She stepped to the trashcan to dispose of the cleaning equipment. Mesmerized by the constant bellows rhythm of the ventilator, she started when another nurse stuck her head inside the room.

"Dr. Prescott just called. He's ready to see you."

Mallory's foot slipped from the trashcan pedal and the lid slammed shut. A swarm of butterflies took flight in her stomach. The tall, dark, and intimidating medical director would see her now. With carved features, a strong nose, and cobalt blue eyes that penetrated straight to her core, J.T. Prescott was the stuff fantasies were made of. She wished she'd never allowed herself to imagine how it might feel to make love to him— especially now, as he was her boss.

How would she face him without turning a deep shade of red? She hated her telling redhead-and-freckles complexion. Would he know what she was thinking?

"It used to be we could approach him right here on the ward and talk about our problems while we did patient care and he made rounds." Mallory removed the dirty gloves and tossed them into the can. "Now we've got to make appointments."

As always, she'd give her all to make sure that everyone was happy. This time her all would be for her fellow nurses. With her luck she'd go all blotchy and perspire above her upper lip while doing it, but face Dr. Prescott she would. She straightened her shoulders and held her head high, willing a wave of confidence to take hold.

"Yeah? Well, he used to be a heck of a lot nicer, too," the other nurse said. "Remember we used to draw straws to see who got to assist him with any bedside procedures?"

Mallory cracked a smile. "I think you used to cheat."

"Who, me?" The other nurse grinned back. "I think he preferred working with you, anyway."

"Oh, yeah, right." Fluttery fingers searched for any stray tendrils of hair from around her face and down her long braid. Could everyone tell she'd had a crush on him?

Back then she'd never considered him as someone to flirt with because he'd been married and out of bounds. Yet still there was something about him that revved up her heart rate whenever he was around.

"He sure isn't the same since he took over that suit job, is he?"

Mallory shook her head. "It's too bad." She remembered how kind and caring he'd been to patients, and how once she'd sworn if she ever got sick she'd want him as her doctor. Had it been the job or the divorce that'd gotten the best of him? She slapped her hands together. "OK. Can you cover my patients while I'm gone?"

The nurse screwed up her face in protest. "I've already got five patients assigned today. How am I supposed to take your four patients? Especially the two ventilators?"

"I've assessed everyone, done a.m. care and passed the meds. There's just one IV antibiotic left for Room 5005."

Pumping the instant sanitizer dispenser on the wall, Mallory scrubbed her hands with the gel in a brisk and frustrated manner.

"Maybe you can take care of the ambulatory patients and I'll ask someone else to cover the vents?"

The other nurse didn't budge from her stance.

"Look, you guys asked me to talk to Dr. Prescott and I'm doing it on *everyone's* behalf, so the least you can do is cover my patients." Damn. The strain of understaffing had everyone at each other's throats. She brushed past her co-worker, made an abrupt stop in the nurses' station and raised her voice so the other four nurses could hear. "Can someone watch my vent patients while I talk to the boss?"

Amidst the clatter and routine chaos, the newest RN on the ward raised her hand from her stool perch while charting. "Sure thing. All for one and one for all, right?"

Thank heavens for bright-eyed optimism. Misguided though it might be. Mallory smiled, remembering how she'd felt the same way fifteen years earlier when she'd first started out in nursing, first as a licensed vocational nurse and a few years later as a registered nurse. Back then, before Dr. Prescott had married, she'd had a whopping crush on him, but who hadn't? For years they'd had a terrific working relationship. Now she hardly knew him any more.

"Thanks. Wish me luck."

"Good luck," everyone chimed in, in a hopeful chorus.

Heading for the bank of elevators down the hall, Mallory recalled how wonderful Dr. Prescott used to be on the ward. Hell, he could pull off any procedure, and he was always personable, too. His patients used to watch him with adoring confidence in their eyes when he discussed his medical decisions and recommendations with them.

On Friday mornings he used to bring the nurses a huge bag of fresh bagels, just as a way to say thanks for all of their good care for his patients. Everyone had liked him. And Mallory's little crush had kindled into a huge and secret fantasy.

These days, he only showed up on Ward Five West with a stern look and a list of complaints in hand. And since his divorce he'd become even colder and harder to reach. JT liked to be in control of things, and she guessed his divorce had thrown him off balance.

She could only guess which man she'd face today—the great guy she'd once worked with, or the intense and humorless medical director? Using all of her resolve to look confident and determined, she turned and smiled for the bright and eager faces of her fellow nurses who'd just waved and wished her good luck.

Under her breath, and beneath a forced grin, she said, "I'm going to need it."

"Come." The baritone voice of J.T. Prescott resonated when Mallory rapped on his office door.

She pushed through the doorway and momentarily stood still, taking everything in. He sat tall behind a large oak desk, busily using every spare moment to sign off on yet a few more papers. Suddenly she remembered just how imposing of a figure he cut.

"Sit," he said, without looking up.

Wearing a black silky-looking knit polo shirt without his usual white coat, she was surprised by his strong and fit arms. He made a jab at his coal-black hair with a few silver threads woven through it, as though searching for the perfect wording to end his report. She'd forgotten how much she liked his strong, aquiline nose.

"I'll be right with you," he said.

Grateful to sit, so her knees would quit quaking, Mallory did as she was told. Up until a year ago, he'd been out of bounds and her unrequited pining—right, more like lustful wishes—had been just that. Now, however, she had to admit she felt particularly vulnerable to his charm. But too bad he hadn't any charm left. All that remained of the man she remembered was his good looks. She forced her glance away before he could look up and find her gawking at him.

Gorgeous framed photographs of scenery from around the world, both in black and white and color, lined his office walls. She'd heard photography was one of his hobbies. One striking red cliff from the Grand Canyon rim caught her attention. How in the world had anyone managed to snap that shot? Having heard of Dr. Prescott's escapades at the hospital water cooler, she figured he'd probably taken it suspended from an airplane upside down, or while skydiving.

He still hadn't looked up.

Mallory took the opportunity to study him more. She'd always been fascinated with his long fingers and strong hands and wondered if he played the piano. Octaves and arpeggios would be a cinch for someone with a reach like that.

Chastising herself for not focusing on why she was there, she glanced away and discovered a picture of a dark-haired boy on his desk. He looked pre-teen and full of mischief, with wild black hair and an elfin smile. It had to be his son.

While she skipped back and forth between father and son, Dr. Prescott lifted his head and impaled her with an intense blue stare. Her world stopped for an instant. She forced herself to breathe.

He plopped his elbows on the desk, fisted one hand inside the other, rested his chin on top, and gave her an all-business look. "We'll have to be brief because I'm leaving tonight for Kenya and still have a million things to do. What brings you here, Mallory?"

Why had she agreed to be the sacrificial lamb for all of the nurses again?

Frantically chasing after every thought rushing

out of her brain, Mallory bit her lower lip and forced herself to focus.

"Nurse staffing."

"Hasn't the hospital addressed this issue before?"

"Not to everyone's satisfaction."

He offered a telling look—must they go through this old story again? Being the sole purpose of her appointment, she ignored his expression and forged ahead.

"As a group, the nurses of Five West are deeply concerned about patient safety under the current conditions. They've asked me to speak to you about it."

When had he changed? He'd once been the perfect doctor, with impeccable beside manners and a caring heart. Now he was nothing more than a strikingly good-looking man with a dead stare behind a desk. Mallory missed the doctor and man she'd known on the wards.

Great. Just what he needed, another headache before he could take off on his long overdue vacation.

This trip would be the first since his divorce, and he intended to enjoy every second of the three-week photography safari in East Africa.

And now Miss Perky Redhead, Mallory Glenn from Five West, insisted on robbing him of more of his precious time. But as Medical Director of L.A. Mercy Hospital, it went with the territory.

He tossed his pen on the desk and leaned back in his chair.

"OK. Shoot, Mallory."

She looked taken aback. Her large amber eyes widened and she went pale. Oh, hell, that wasn't how he'd meant to come off. He briefly considered searching his drawer for an ammonia ampoule in case she passed out. But she didn't give him a chance. The color returned to her cheeks in record time and blossomed to bright red.

"We on Five West feel understaffed. There is evidence regarding the relationship between nurse staffing and rates of hospital-acquired infection, urinary-tract infections, and pressure ulcers," she said, leaning forward in her chair, fingers fidgeting.

"And the evidence is not compelling," he added.

Mallory locked eyes with him, and it pleasantly surprised him. She'd always been straightforward and sincere—it had been something he'd particularly liked about her—but why did she seem nothing less than stubborn today?

"We currently have two nurses injured on duty, one indefinitely off the job. And our rate of incident reports for unusual occurrences, patient falls, and medication errors has increased over the last three months."

"Nurses get injured because of poor body mechanics. Mercy Hospital sends you to annual updates, yet nurses still manage to throw out your backs."

"When you have a two-hundred-pound patient suddenly fall on you, there is no such thing as *proper* body mechanics. The goal is to keep the patients safe and to get them back in bed. Our backs pay the price."

"Correct me if I'm wrong, but don't we have a hospital lift team?"

She squinted and shot him a contemptuous look—one that said, You just don't get it since you've left bedside care, do you?—then quickly worked to cover it up—doing a poor job, he noted.

"It isn't always in the patients' best interest to leave them lying on the floor while we wait for the lift team to materialize. Not to mention how that must look to other patients and their visitors."

OK, so he was a bit out of touch with patient care these days, but really she was acting as if it were the end of health care as they knew it in the twenty-first century.

What had started as a routine meeting had turned into a heated debate. He was a skilled and highly paid professional, and he knew how to de-escalate tension. But he felt particularly wiped out today, maybe because of everything he'd been doing lately—hospital administration, constant meetings for the new rehab wing, making father-son bonding time, and vacation planning.

He'd felt especially exhausted when he'd made out the huge alimony and child support check earlier. His ex-wife had raked him over the coals in their divorce settlement, and now she was fighting for full custody of their ten-year-old son, Corey, so she could get even more money.

No way would he let that happen. He intended to stay involved in his son's life and that meant having him live at least fifty per cent of the time with him. Someday he hoped to have Corey accompany him on his trips. The boy already showed an uncanny eye for photography. But…

Focus, Prescott.

"Let's back up. What is the current patient-to-nurse ratio on Five West?"

"In writing? Or reality?"

"Both."

"As you know, we are considered a general medical-surgical ward, therefore our numbers are supposed to be one nurse to four patients. Yet we seem to be the dump-on-us ward. Frequently we are short-staffed, and everyone has to take as many as five patients, and occasionally, when we have a late-shift admission, six patients. It's killing us."

"That's a bit extreme, isn't it?"

"Two of my patients are long-term ventilator patients, yet I still have to take four patients when it should be three, max. Three of the other nurses have five patients today because our ward is full. Our nursing supervisor couldn't spare an extra nurse. It's a joke to even think about giving patient education. No one has time."

She paused just long enough to make sure he was listening. He assumed his most studious expression.

"Last week we had a near code blue."

He watched her, digesting what she'd said. She'd pulled her long, thick braid over her shoulder and wrapped and unwrapped the bottom of the red tendrils around her fingers in a nervous yet intriguing manner. He'd always wondered how her shiny, silky hair felt.

"The patient had become short of breath and used the bedside call light. We were all so busy that it was several minutes before anyone went into the room. By that time his lips were blue and his cheeks mottled. His oxygen sats were in the high eighties. He could have gone into respiratory arrest. I shudder to think what could have happened if I'd gone in a minute later."

Her cheeks were hot with color, her hands had balled into fists, and an earnest gold glint had appeared in her eyes. She wasn't asking about more money, she was asking for better staffing. Why? Because she cared about the patients. Well, so did he. Hadn't patient care been foremost on his mind when he'd been the attending doctor? But he also had a budget to balance, especially with the drain of the new rehab construction project. And his statistics didn't bear out what she'd claimed.

"I can only tell you, Ms. Glenn, that there is no hard and fast evidence that the number of staff RNs affects hospital mortality or the rates of hospital acquired pneumonia or, for that matter, the number of RNs and hours worked adding to or subtracting from hospital length of stay."

"We work in the real world, Dr. Prescott. When you used to work at the bedside, you understood. Now your statistics can't possibly explain why more nurses are getting burned out on our ward. But if you must quote statistics, I've got a few of my own." She gave an agitated scratch at her pert nose.

Being in vacation mode, it occurred to him that he enjoyed watching her. If he was honest with himself, he'd admit he'd always enjoyed looking at Mallory Glenn.

"Studies show that increasing the number of RNs on any given ward doesn't appear to increase hospital costs. In fact, it may even decrease costs when you factor in the extreme expense of adverse patient outcomes with lower nurse-to-patient ratios requiring more extensive treatments."

So his latest debate opponent had come prepared. He liked a good sparring partner— they normally made good lovers. And he'd always had a soft spot for redheads—his very first girlfriend had been one. There was something fragile and alluring about Mallory he couldn't quite put his finger on, though when it came to nursing she was a diligent and competent nurse, anything but fragile. He'd always seen her give expert patient care on the wards. And he'd also always enjoyed watching her walk from behind.

If his mind was wandering to her face and figure, he must be losing the debate. Either that, or it had been too long since he'd had a woman in his arms. His lips almost twitched into a smile. Maybe he was losing ground—he'd use his best defense. "OK. We'll do a study on your ward. I'll get on it the minute I return from my vacation."

"But we need extra help now, not next month."

"I'll approve overtime. If anyone wants to work extra shifts, they may."

He felt the need to shake out his feet. He'd been sitting in his chair for so many hours, having meetings and doing last-minute paperwork, that they'd gone to sleep. He tried to stretch out his legs, but his feet moved like dead weights.

"Well, when you do your study," she said with clear frustration in her voice, "I suggest you consider both nurse and patient satisfaction surveys. We're slipping in patient satisfaction, and we're losing perfectly good nurses to our competitors because of better working conditions." She swept a long, milky-white arm through the air, making an exasperated gesture. "And in case you haven't noticed, there is a nursing shortage in California. Quality of patient care is an issue that can't be ignored."

With fire kindling in her eyes, Mallory wouldn't leave without being invited. He'd have to use the old stand-up-to-announce-this-meeting-is-over trick. He rolled back his chair and pushed himself to stand. His feet and lower legs felt like dead tree stumps. He eased himself back into his chair, attempting to hide his concern.

"Is something wrong, Dr. Prescott?"

"I'm fine. Just getting antsy to leave for my vacation." He'd try his male charm to lure her out of his office. "May we pick this meeting back up in, say…" he looked at his watch "…three weeks and one day?" He cocked his head, raised his brows, and smiled.

She disguised her disappointment with grace. Her glance swept downward toward her lap, as though she was weighing up the proposition. Thick brown lashes almost touched her cheeks. She pursed pink gloss-covered lips while she thought.

He felt compelled to offer a crumb of hope.

"Mallory, I promise to give the staffing issue my undivided attention as soon as I get back.

I'll be rested and raring to go. In the mean-time, you have an opportunity to make some extra money."

Priding himself on knowing his staff, he knew that once upon a time Mallory Glenn had been a teenage single mother. And now, barely looking over thirty but having to be several years older than that, she had a child ready for college and no husband to help defray the costs. Surely she could use the extra hours and overtime pay.

She'd caught his drift and prepared to stand. She nodded at him and stretched her mouth into a satisfying smile—the nicest thing he'd seen all day. "I'm going to hold you to it, Dr. Prescott. For old times' sake."

He grinned as she nervously played with her braid. "It's a deal. For old times' sake. If my feet hadn't gone to sleep on me, I'd see you out, but…"

"That's fine." She turned to leave, and he watched her slender legs walk toward the door, legs that could be downright striking given sexier shoes than those dowdy crêpe-soled nurses' clogs. A narrow waist and shapely hips filled out the uniform skirt in a most intriguing manner. At least something he'd always considered pleasant on the job hadn't changed.

Get a life, Prescott. Better yet, find a date.

Disappointed, Mallory closed the door to Dr. Prescott's office and leaned on her hands against the wall. The time had been they could chat and make jokes with each other. Now he'd become so far removed that she hardly recognized him.

Had she made any headway? He'd changed so much since he'd become the medical director. They used to be on the same team. Now she was sure his allegiance went to the business side of medicine instead of patients. She bit her lip and thought how she'd word the lack of progress for her co-workers.

"He has promised to look into it next month."

Yeah, that would go down well.

A loud thud from inside his office caught her attention. It sounded as if furniture had been upended. The scuffling continued, and she heard a strained curse.

Curiosity drove her to knock on the door. "Dr. Prescott? Are you all right?" Without waiting for a response, she swung the door open and found him on the floor with a baffled look on his face.

Mallory rushed to him. "What happened? Did you pass out? Are you OK?"

He shook his head and alarm radiated from his face. "I can't walk."

She gasped. "Shall I call the code assist team?"

"No! I'll probably be fine. I just need to get the circulation back in my legs. A few minutes ago they felt like pins and needles. But now they're completely dead."

Lifting the legs of his slacks, she felt his skin. It was warm. She felt the popliteal pulse behind his knee, then pushed down his sock and felt the pulse on the top of one foot, then the other. They both checked out fine. She flicked her finger on his shin. "Can you feel that?"

He lifted a brow and shook his head, concern in his eyes.

She scanned the room and considered helping him back into his rolling desk chair and taking him to the ER for evaluation. Realizing how ridiculous that would look, she said, "I'm going to find a wheelchair. Wait right here."

"No!"

"Yes! Don't be ridiculous."

She tore down the hall, heading for the employee elevator bank where extra equipment was often left behind. Thankful to find an unclaimed wheelchair, she pushed it back to his office and right up beside him. She locked the brakes.

"Here, let me help you up."

Being a tall and sturdy man, she knew the lift would be difficult without his help.

"Easy," he said. "Don't hurt your back."

As inappropriate a time to laugh as it was, a soft chuckle escaped her lips. "Don't worry, I've attended the annual body mechanics update. It covers everything."

He tossed her a deadpan stare. "Point well taken."

He turned to a hands-and-knees position with his hair falling into his face. "I can get myself into the chair."

Mallory fought the urge to brush the hair out of his eyes, but instead let him struggle to help himself up. When his legs wouldn't co-operate, she used her own strength and pushed against his rear end to help him move into the wheelchair. He climbed up, twisted and turned, then sat, noticeably out of breath, as though he carried a sack of bricks. One by one, she lifted each leg to place them onto the footrests.

"Come on, Dr. Prescott," she said. "Let's get you down to Emergency."

They rolled through the emergency-room doors in record time. When the staff ER doc saw who the patient was, he jumped to action.

"What happened, JT?"

"He can't walk," Mallory blurted out.

Dr. Prescott scrubbed his face with a hand, then studied it with a surprised look in his eyes. "Now my hands feel tingly, like my legs did earlier."

"Let's get him on a gurney. Oxygen. Get him some oxygen."

A nurse appeared from across the room and swept open the curtain to one of the ER cubicles. Mallory rolled the wheelchair beside the bed.

With a sudden spurt of energy, JT made a desperate gymnast's attempt—using straightened arms, as if mounting a pommel horse—to lift his bottom halfway out of the seat. Mallory grabbed and supported his legs. The other nurse held him around the waist and pulled him across the wheelchair armrest and onto the gurney.

Mallory hooked him up to the oxygen on the wall, then stood back to allow the ER nurse to take over. The doctor hit him with a barrage of rapid-fire questions.

"When did the symptoms begin? Any recent injuries? Any unexplained fevers? How has the blood pressure been? Any relevant family history for similar symptoms?"

JT kept shaking his head in a bewildered manner and answered, "Just today. No. I don't know. Fine. I don't think so."

Having done her duty for Dr. Prescott, and considering the short-staffed nursing team on Five West, Mallory decided she'd better return to her ward. She walked toward the bed, took his hand and looked him straight in the eyes with a worried glance.

JT held her gaze, and gave a stoic nod.

Who knew where he'd be or how he would have gotten down here without her?

"Thank you, Mallory." His palm pressed over her hand. "I'll be fine."

She blinked and gave him a reassuring smile, then tried to convince herself she believed what she was about to say.

"I'm sure you'll be fine, too."

CHAPTER TWO

HOW DEPENDABLE was the hospital grapevine? By the time Mallory returned to work the next day, rumors about JT were running wild. Could she believe them?

"Did you hear about Dr. Prescott?" one of the nurses at report asked Mallory.

Respectful of patient privacy, she hadn't mentioned what had happened yesterday to anyone. "I know he wasn't feeling well. Is he OK?" She dreaded what the nurse's response might be.

"He's in the ICU on a ventilator."

Stunned, she blindly grasped for a chair and sat. "What?"

"They think he has Guillain-Barré syndrome."

Wasn't that an inflammatory disorder of the peripheral nerves? If she remembered her pathophysiology correctly, it usually occurred after a viral or bacterial infection, and had a rapid onset of weakness or paralysis of the legs and arms, but under extreme circumstances could also spread to the breathing muscles. Looking back, he'd had all of those symptoms. And now he was on a ventilator.

"GBS? How did he get it? Did he have flu recently? Or an intestinal disorder?"

"I don't know, but he's hanging on for dear life right now."

Feeling as though she'd been kicked in the solar plexus and the wind had been knocked out of her, Mallory gasped. "Oh, my God."

A nest of anxiety lodged in her chest and kept her distracted during change of shift report. With sincere intentions of stopping by and checking on him later, if for no other reason than to ease her mind, she prepared for her work day. But a long and grueling shift ensued, and soon becoming completely distracted with another kind of stress, the hospital bedside visit she'd planned to Dr. Prescott never happened.

Yet she worried about him daily. Knowing the ICU only allowed family members to visit, she made a habit of stopping by each morning before starting work to chat with her friends. The sketchy updates on the doctor were never good. And the rules on patient confidentiality remained strict. No visitors. No specifics about his condition could be given. Though with quick glances into his room when she passed, she could see he was still on a ventilator.

As the days went on Mallory had time to put their relationship into perspective. Just because she had been the one who had found him in his office, JT wasn't really any of her business. Since he'd changed jobs they no longer had a daily working relationship. Fact was, she had nothing to do with his life whatsoever, and the only thing he had to do with hers was to sign her paychecks.

Besides, Mallory had realistic worries of her own to deal with, such as how was she going to pay for her daughter's college tuition in the fall?

Over the next two weeks she allowed herself to become consumed with her life. One day, she forgot to ask about Dr. Prescott, and the next she heard he'd been transferred home.

* * *

Mallory's daughter—seventeen-year-old Morgan—sat across from Mallory at the breakfast table. Pale and delicate, she'd pulled her dark blonde hair back into a stretch band, and without an ounce of make-up on looked closer to fourteen.

"You've done your part. You've taken the tough classes and maintained straight As." Mallory sipped her morning coffee and tried to think how to phrase what she was about to say. "I knew this day would come, but I haven't prepared the way I should've."

With large hopeful eyes Morgan spoke up. "But I got those two scholarships to help."

"I know, sweetie, but that college back east is way out of my budget."

At thirty-five, and being a single mother, Mallory knew how to work hard. She'd done it all her life, but this dream of her daughter's was going to cost a lot more than she'd ever imagined.

The disappointed look in Morgan's eyes when she handed back the college application made her throat tighten. Did she want to stomp on Morgan's dream the way she'd ruined her own?

Not on her life. She grabbed back the application.

"Look, you keep saving your part-time job money and keep applying for those scholarships. I'll work more and look into loans. We'll get you there."

Morgan jumped up from her chair, rushed to Mallory's side and threw her arms around her neck. "I love you, Mom. You're the greatest mom in the world."

Loving every second but not wanting to come off as a pushover, she kept a stern look on her face. "You'd better keep your grades up in college. I don't want to hear anything about wild parties or binge drinking or…"

Morgan kept kissing her cheeks and squeezing her shoulders. Mallory pretended to get annoyed. "Stop it, you're messing up my hair. I've got to go to work."

"I can't wait to tell my friends I get to move to Rhode Island for college!"

After Mallory had eaten lunch at work, she perused the bulletin board in the nurses' lounge.

She feared the prospect of her daughter moving across the country and leaving her with an empty nest. What would it be like to live alone? She was also in need of extra money—a lot of extra money.

Seventeen years of doting on Morgan were coming to an end. Mallory wouldn't have any more excuses for her near non-existent social life. An extra job seemed like the logical solution.

Her eyes came to rest on a typed notice, which read, "Seeking a qualified registered nurse for weekend relief; bedside home care. Twelve-hour shifts preferred, 9 a.m. or 9 p.m. Saturday, Sunday, or both weekend shifts. $50.00/hr."

She did the math and rushed down the hall to Personnel. When she arrived, one major dilemma almost kept her from applying for the job.

The patient was none other than J.T. Prescott, the man she'd had a major crush on for years, and beside that he was her boss.

But the money was too good, and she knew how to care for ventilator patients, so she signed on for both weekend days, every weekend.

When she got back to her ward, Jenny, the newest RN, sat beside her to do some paperwork. "You look worried. Is everything OK?"

Mallory sighed. "I've just applied for a weekend job."

"This place doesn't wear you out enough?"

"My daughter wants to go back east for college, so I'll need all the money I can get my hands on."

"But what about the quality of your life? You can't work twenty-four seven."

"I don't exactly have a life anyway. In the last three years I've gone on, let's see, one, two, three dates. I'll spare you the details."

Jenny laughed. "I could tell you some horror stories myself." She grew serious and patted Mallory's hand. "But as far as nursing goes, you're my role model. I really look up to you. I just want you to know that."

"Thanks, Miss Green-Behind-The-Ears. I wish you'd tell Administration that, so they'd give me a raise."

She grinned then grew serious. She put down her pen and thought about her fifteen-plus years in the nursing profession. It hadn't been such a bad haul. At eighteen she'd had a daughter to be responsible for, so she'd taken the quickest path to cash and became a licensed vocational nurse. When most of her friends had been going to frat parties and cramming for finals, she'd planned Morgan's first birthday party and got her first job. When supporting her and her daughter on an LVN's salary hadn't cut the budget, she returned to nursing school when Morgan had started kindergarten.

It felt gratifying to know that her nursing peers respected her. She loved patient care—it seemed to come second nature to her. She loved being a mom, too, but times and things had changed. With a million little thoughts threatening to keep her distracted from her work, she scrubbed at her face. And before she could indulge in one more, a patient call light went off. She jumped up to answer it.

Walking across the ward, she wondered if she could handle both her regular job and the home-care job, not to mention working seven days a week. Did she have a choice?

It was a very tough route that she'd only be able to sustain for a limited time.

She entered the patient's room.

Maybe Dr. Prescott wouldn't make it. What a horrible thought. Could she handle it if he didn't? Or maybe he'd get better. Who knew? She preferred to focus on the positive.

The room felt like a cave, cold and dark—something she'd imagined in a Dickens novel when she'd read it in seventh grade. The hospital-style bed and extra equipment cluttered the room and took up half of the space. A single brown leather chair and ottoman with a floor lamp and small table sat tucked in the corner for the caregiver. The ventilator hummed and clicked and stammered each time the patient hacked.

Mallory ventured toward the end of the bed. According to the chart, J.T. Prescott had been home for one month. "I'm so sorry about everything that's happened to you," she said, mostly to herself.

Could this patient possibly be the same tall, robust, and confident medical director she'd known from Mercy Hospital? Could this shadow of life be the same man that had demanded her attention just by his mere presence, any time he'd visited the hospital ward? He looked more like a recluse than the dashing dark-haired Dr. Prescott.

It had been six weeks since their meeting in his office.

At a loss how to begin, she walked to the window and threw open the curtains to allow the natural light of day inside. "The sun will either begin your healing process or, if you're a vampire, fry you." Going for a bit of humor, she turned to catch any reaction. There was none.

Well, he looked pale enough to be a vampire. His eyes twitched and blinked and fought with the invading rays of sun and he let go with a paroxysm of silent ventilator coughing, setting off the alarm. Did he even recognize her? Or had he withdrawn completely into the prison of his paralyzed body?

Mallory closed the curtain halfway and approached the bedside to suction his tracheostomy. She vowed to use saline lavage every hour to thin and clear his airway secretions, hoping it would make a difference.

"Do you like music?" Cringing that she'd asked him a question when he couldn't talk, she plunged ahead. "I'll bring a radio tomorrow and we'll find a nice station."

Dull crusty gray eyes had replaced the vibrant blue she'd remembered.

He looked so pitiful, lying there tethered to a breathing machine, feeding tube, urinary catheter, and intravenous line, the sum total of his being. All perfect entryways for opportunistic infection, and he was helpless to stop it. She knew it was like fighting a wild fire with a wet towel for nurses to prevent certain infections from developing in patients such as him.

She'd do her best to create a cheerful atmosphere for the man she remembered and respected, despite the overwhelming surge of depression that passed through her.

"Don't suppose you want to hear all the latest gossip from Mercy Hospital, do you?" She shook her head and smiled down at him. "I didn't think so. I'll shut up now."

Mallory looked at the man before her, pale, gaunt, frail, oily and dry, all at once. He needed mouth care and once she'd finished with his suctioning, she planned to do just that. In fact, she intended to give him a complete bed bath and wash his hair before the morning was over. Today, she would definitely earn her money.

The night-shift nurse had told her about the long list of dos and don'ts posted on the wall. The paper read, 'The Patient's Bill of Rights and Wishes.' She read them a second time.

"What idiot thought up these?" She spoke out loud to her patient.

He furrowed his brow and sent her dagger looks.

"And what genius had the bright idea to send you home from the hospital after two short weeks?" She waltzed over to Dr. Prescott. "Can you believe it? I know California is sending patients home sooner than they are ready, but this takes the cake. When you're better, you should file a complaint against the hospital. Better yet, a lawsuit."

She thought she detected a low growl from his throat. Suddenly distracted, she heard footsteps creak down the wooden floor of the hallway. She stopped cold in her monologue and listened.

"Isn't it frightening to be alone here all the time?" She shivered just as the door opened.

A man with a weathered face and grizzled hair, in a gray uniform, stuck his head inside. "Good morning. My name's Jake." He reached for Mallory's hand and shook it. "I've worked for Dr. Prescott as his grounds keeper and security guard for the last five years. It's just me and him around here now," he said in a gravelly voice.

He stepped inside the room. "Hiya, Doc." He lifted a hand, like taking an oath, and acknowledged his boss.

"He don't have any relatives to take care of him. Heaven forbid his ex-wife might step up to the plate to help out. No. She couldn't put a crimp in her social life the good Dr. Prescott here pays for."

The old man smiled toward the bed with a hint of blue visible beneath his drooping lids, and Mallory thought she saw JT's strained face muscles relax.

"How could the Mercy Hospital discharge

planning team send him home to an empty house?"

"They had no choice. Dr. Prescott here has everything written down. He's not to stay in any hospital for more than two weeks. His wishes. His lawyer threatened to take it to court if they gave him any guff. This one here likes to be in charge, and he's got everything written out." He walked toward the door. "Just like these rules here. He thought through all of this when he wrote his directives out a long time ago."

Mallory blanched, remembering her earlier comment.

"Dr Berger comes every day to check up on him, and so does a respiratory therapist. There's twenty-four-hour round-the-clock bedside care. He specified only RNs should be hired and trusted the head of Mercy Hospital Personnel to find the best ones. I live on the premises. I've got a hotline to both the fire department and the police. Everything is all worked out."

He stepped toward the exit and made a rat-a-tap-tap with arthritic fingers on the wall. "He's his own man, he is." He winked a pouchy eye. "So I guess I'll be seeing you around?"

This ancient yet alert man was the person J.T. Prescott trusted with his very life. She guessed she could trust him, too.

"Every weekend."

"Call if you need me." He nodded, handed her his pager number and left.

Slowly putting it all together, she realized J.T. Prescott was a total control freak to go to such extremes to have extensive and thorough advance directives for his personal medical care. Yet wasn't that what all hospitals and doctors recommended these days?

The horror of his helpless condition sank in. How must a man used to being in charge and running things feel being trapped inside his body?

She turned to face him, completely aware of the video camera security system sweeping the room. No doubt Dr. Prescott had hired a security company to make sure no one abused him in the event he wound up like this. He'd probably written that part out, too. He'd thought of absolutely everything.

"Don't worry. Since it's basically just you and me, I'm going to be your personal advocate every weekend. Since you can't speak and I can, I'll sum it all up for you. Un-freaking-believable. That's what your situation is." After a surge of emotion she pushed some stray hairs away from her face, and worked to regain her composure. "I promise to take good care of you." She brushed oily hair off his forehead and smiled down at him. "Now, pardon me while I fill the basin and give you a bed bath."

She heard him break into another coughing spasm when she turned away.

His full and complete life had come down to this, a mere existence monitored by machines and strangers. He should have been in Kenya, snapping pictures of strange wildlife. The only thing strange in this room was him.

But right this moment strong fingers were touching his head, massaging shampoo into his hair, invigorating the only senses he had left.

The nurse he knew as the perky Mallory Glenn washed and scrubbed his head with warm water and scalp-tingling shampoo. Her fingertips felt like angel kisses, and he kept his eyes tightly shut so she wouldn't be able to tell how she moved him. His head and face being the only place left on his body he could feel, her stroking caused chills down his neck. So starved for human contact, her touch danced right to his core. Which was strange, as theoretically he couldn't feel anything below his neck. Yet he felt phantom electrical sparks across his body, and wondered if his paralyzed flesh could still make goose-bumps on his limbs.

Wait. He had feeling back in his face. He made some exaggerated facial expressions to make sure. A big clown-like smile. A pouting frown. Eyes stretched wide, then tightly shut. He hadn't been able to do that yesterday. Progress! If he could laugh, he would.

Man could not live by machine alone. Human contact was vital to his existence and he savored the feel of Mallory's touch. Elated by the sudden small steps toward progress, he gave in to her spell. She washed and stroked his head with relaxing warm water, and he wanted to groan, but he fought the spontaneous response.

After the invigorating ministrations, maybe he'd forgive her for accusing him of being an idiot.

Why should he be called an idiot? Was man not the author of his own existence? Then why was it so far-fetched to dictate his wishes about medical care should a time such as this arise?

He only wished his father had done the same thing before he'd had a massive stroke and had lain in a prolonged vegetative state, being kept alive by machines, until he'd finally died. The lawyers hadn't been able to work fast enough through the court system to have his plug pulled.

JT shuddered to think what would have happened to him had he not put everything in writing. He'd have been left to rot in a skilled nursing facility—one of many lives run by machines. Wasn't that the point of building the rehab wing for the hospital—to have a place with skilled personnel for those in need of special care but not acute enough to remain in hospital?

At least he knew here, at home, if his paralysis continued as it was, his trusted grounds keeper, Jake, would have the authority to make decisions.

Everything had been spelled out far in advance of his becoming ill in a secret letter that only Jake possessed. They had an understanding, which he paid Jake well for. JT could breathe easier knowing that he wouldn't be left in limbo, that was, if he couldn't breathe on his own in another month.

Resting assured that everything had been committed in writing, he closed his eyes and allowed himself to enjoy every stroke of Mallory's skilled fingers.

Her strong and talented hands almost lulled him to sleep. Feeling safe and secure in her care, he would have welcomed a nap.

No such luck.

Once JT was clean, Mallory lathered his skin with lotion, lifting and bending each joint of his body. She knew he'd specified no massages with oil on his list, but she didn't give a damn. His skin needed it, and if it got too dry, it could crack, break down, and become infected. She had a duty to her patient that overrode his misguided wishes.

His body had already stiffened up, and she was damned if she would ever let JT develop contractures of his joints or pull inward to a fetal position on her watch.

She started on his feet, and rolled the ankle joint around in its socket. Then worked up his leg.

"There we go. Back and forth. Back and forth. Your muscles are craving this. I can tell."

Mallory was shocked by his loss of muscle mass. He'd always been athletic and well developed, and she'd often passed him on the stairwell at work, skipping up the flights, barely out of breath, as if it were nothing. She remembered the strong arms she'd noticed that day in his office. Now all of his strength had been zapped by complete bedrest.

"In case you're wondering why I took this job, my daughter is getting ready for college. She's a great student, and I want to give her every opportunity I can. Thank God she got my brains and not her IQ-of-lettuce father's. Not that I'm bitter or anything," she said, poking her tongue in her cheek.

She pushed inward and bent his knee toward the center of his body, covering his groin with a bath towel, respectful of his privacy. She'd done everything in her power not to gape when she'd bathed him. She was a paid professional, and bathing patients was part of what she did. She'd seen thousands of men in her lifetime as a nurse.

But JT was the man for whom she'd carried a secret torch for ever. He was the kind of man she imagined she could find for herself one day, if she only stayed vigilant. Now he lay before her weak and helpless, yet something in his eyes remained proud. Was there a place for their prior friendship here in this dark and dreary room? The fact that he'd refused to look at her once when she'd cleaned him drove the point home that they had a unique relationship.

"Yeah. So you'll be seeing a lot of me for a while. Hopefully you'll be out of this bed soon, and back to work, Dr. Prescott."

Working firmly yet gently, she pressed against

the decreased range of motion. "We could use more good docs like you on the wards."

She repeated the same pattern on the other side of his body, and finally worked her way up to his hands and arms.

She rubbed and stretched each finger, lacing her own through his and bending gently backward at the wrist. A subtle chill ran up her arm with the intimate intertwining of their fingers. Humming quietly, she massaged his forearms and worked his elbow joints. She leaned over him, lifted and tugged on his entire arm, away from the socket and around in a half-circle, then reversed it.

They'd never been this close before. Granted, she'd imagined being skin to skin with him, but before today they'd never even touched.

She noticed the strangest look in his eyes when she finished her therapy.

She smiled at him and his forehead unfurled.

"Tomorrow I'll have you doing calisthenics." Mallory grinned and patted his hand when she laid it gently across his chest. "It's almost time for lunch."

She moved away from the bedside and found the cans of protein formula to bolus into his stomach tube.

As she poured his liquid lunch into the feeding pouch, on the kangaroo pump, she wondered what kind of man would take the time to think through every step of his potential demise.

J.T. Prescott had.

Mallory ate her brown-bag lunch and put her feet up on the leather ottoman during her break. JT slept peacefully, and she didn't want to wake him, though soon it would be time to reposition him to avoid skin breakdown. No way would she allow him to develop bedsores while he was in her care.

Was it her or had something strange passed between them when she'd washed his hair? It seemed as though he was feeling things for the first time. The prickling flesh across his body couldn't be ignored. She'd caused a reaction in him. His thick black hair had grown to near shoulder-length, and she'd loved running her fingers through it. She'd fantasized about that once upon a time, but had never dreamed it would happen under these horrid circumstances.

A sudden curiosity to find out more about her boss drove her out of the bedroom and into his living room. As suspected, a baby grand piano was in the corner. Sheet music lay spread across the music holder. She checked the composers—Debussy, Gershwin, Scott Joplin. More of his multitude of personal photographs with stunning vistas graced the intense rust-red painted walls everywhere she looked. His taste in furniture was eclectic, almost bohemian, which surprised but also pleased her. His ex-wife must have gotten all of the decorator-perfect pieces.

Afraid to spend more than a minute or two away from his bedside and her duty, she decided to head back into his room, but not before she noticed a wall full of books, many of them medical, and one particular book left open on his desk. *The Day on Fire,* a book based on the life of Arthur Rimbaud, the famous French poet. Hmm. So JT was a man of adventure, music, *and* poetry, not just a controlling, hard-as-nails doctor and hospital medical director. What else, she wondered, was there to discover about him?

Before she left, one other thing nagged at the back of her brain. Guillain-Barré syndrome was supposed to be a condition of ascending and then descending paralysis. She understood the length of the illness was unpredictable, but why had Dr. Prescott remained in this protracted recovery? The medical progress notes in his chart had no definite reason as to why he'd contracted the acute inflammatory paralysis in the first place. Why had his immune system attacked itself? He'd been healthy without viral or bacterial infection for several months prior to being stricken, yet here he lay, helpless and dependent on the kindness of strangers.

Mallory scanned the wall for medical books. Surely somewhere inside one of them there had to be the key about his disease. She also had the internet at her fingertips at home. There had been a bond between them when they'd worked together, and earlier something unique had passed between them. Admitting what she'd sensed as a connection and betting he'd felt it too, she vowed to find out everything she could about the disease and its treatment. Hopefully, if she dug deep enough, she could find a way to help him.

She removed a book from the shelf, *Acute Medical Conditions—Possible Causes and Current Treatments*. She planned to start her quest for saving Dr. Prescott that night.

CHAPTER THREE

AFTER finding nothing of value in the medical book she'd brought home, Mallory turned to the internet. Though both physically and mentally exhausted from her twelve-hour day with JT, she pressed on with bleary eyes.

Fifty per cent of GBS cases were caused by upper respiratory viruses or intestinal bacteria. The virus could change the nature of the cells in the nervous system so that the patient's immune system identified them as foreign cells and attacked the nerve fibers.

She pushed back in her chair.

What caused the other fifty per cent? She thought back to that day in the ER. JT had answered no to both of those questions. What had caused his attack?

She scooted forward, scrolled down the page

bar and dug deeper into the information. Occasionally it occurred after surgery, and more rarely after a vaccination.

Hmm. That was interesting.

Guillain-Barré seemed to be a mysterious autoimmune disease. Neurological scientists, immunologists, virologists, and pharmacologists were all working to learn how to prevent the disorder and to make better therapies available when it struck, yet six weeks after developing his first symptoms, JT remained paralyzed, with no hint of the syndrome receding.

Mallory had no idea what treatments had been given to him when he'd been in the ICU at Mercy Hospital, and she didn't have access to his hospital chart.

She reached for the medical book she'd brought home, and flipped the pages back to what she'd read earlier. It said spinal fluid, the fluid that bathed the spinal cord and brain, would have a higher protein concentration with GBS. It also said there were treatments to speed the recovery along. She wondered if he'd had any of them while in the hospital. Of course he had, hadn't he?

Mallory rubbed her eyes and heard the front door open. So involved in research, she hadn't realized it was only five minutes before Morgan's 1 a.m. curfew.

"Hey, Mom, what are you still doing up?"

"I'm reading about your friends on that internet meat market, Cyber Space," she teased, raising a brow and impaling her daughter with a threatening glare. "I'm not too impressed with that peek-a-boo picture of Crystal."

"As if." Her self-proclaimed "nerd girl" giggled at the prospect of any one of her honors-student friends being on the sometimes wild and raunchy message boards.

Mallory smiled. She couldn't fake out her daughter no matter how much she tried.

The willowy ash blonde with huge green eyes and intentionally smudged liner tossed her woven sac purse onto the couch. She plopped down beside it on the overstuffed pillows, and sighed.

"What's wrong, sweetie?"

"It's kinda sad to think about my friends split-ting up and going to different schools. We all say we'll keep in touch, but I know it'll never be the same." She leaned her head back on the cushions and placed her wrist on her forehead in a melo-dramatic fashion.

Mallory smiled, turned off the computer, and joined her on the couch. She patted her daughter's bony knee.

"High school isn't the end of your life," she said sympathetically. "College is just the beginning. It may test your true friendships, but it will also bring you new friends. Heck, you may even meet the guy you wind up marrying there."

"Mom, I'm going to an all-girls' college, remember?"

Mallory sputtered. "Right."

Morgan became quiet. Mallory yawned. It was hard to believe she had been almost the same age as Morgan was now when she'd given birth—a child with a baby. But, heck, she'd done all right. She'd raised a well-adjusted and bright girl. She could pat herself on the back for that.

"Mom, I want you to know I'm searching for more scholarships. I feel bad that you have to work so much."

"Hey, that's what we parents do. We give you the best chance to spread your wings, then expect you to take care of us when we're old and gray."

"Payback."

"You got that right," Mallory said, and yawned loudly. "Now, I've got to get some sleep. I've got a hot doc to take care of again tomorrow. But speaking of payback, doesn't Crystal work in medical records at Mercy Hospital?"

"Yeah."

"I may need a favor."

Without thinking, she walked to the window and took down the large hanging crystal teardrop. Then she thumbed through her CD collection for some Debussy and found *Clair de Lune* and *La Mer*. She tucked both inside her nurse's bag and grinned at her daughter before heading off to bed.

Morgan rolled her eyes at her. "You are so weird."

It was the last thing she heard before she closed her bedroom door with a smile for her daughter and a plan for her doctor.

* * *

Mallory quietly hung the crystal in the window with a suction cup and stick-on hook. She slipped the CD into the portable player she'd brought and pressed the start button. JT slept peacefully, with the ventilator pulsing out the rhythm of his breaths. The "Afternoon of the Faun" began to play.

Eager to say hello to her patient, Mallory stood beside the bed and watched. She'd put on a bit of mascara and lipstick that morning all the while asking what the heck she thought she was doing. JT was just her patient, and she was only his nurse.

One angry eye cracked open then slammed tightly shut. She planted her hands on her hips, waiting for him to come around.

"Well, good morning to you, too."

He kept his eyes sealed with a squint.

She forced him to turn and did her initial assessment, took his vital signs, checked his subclavian line and stomach tube, and prepared to suction his tracheostomy.

His refusal to respond communicated, Go

away, in no uncertain terms. She understood that sleep was the only thing he had left to control. But it was her duty to not let him forget about life.

The bright summer morning light hit the crystal just right, and cast a beautiful rainbow on the wall.

"Oh, look Dr. Prescott." She repositioned him in the bed so he could see it. One of his ridiculous and strict rules was "No pictures of family at the bedside." Another was "No music." Well, hell, she'd broken so many things on his list already, she had no intention of observing either of those dreary rules.

She'd stopped in his living room before starting her shift and had found pictures of his young son, which she strategically placed around his bed. One was at his eye level.

Finally forced to open his eyes, he noticed the picture of his son just below the rainbow. He looked puzzled, but not displeased. She had no doubt that he heard the music above the ventilator rhythm as well, especially when it swelled in a lovely crescendo.

She smiled and waited for him to do the same. Instead, he glowered.

"You are such a grouch," she said, undaunted, feeling familiar with him perhaps beyond the reality of their relationship. "I swear, some people just want to curl up into little balls and die. Well, not on my shift, buddy." She playfully pushed his shoulder with her hand. "Isn't that what you'd have said to one of your patients back at Mercy Hospital if they'd have given you this same attitude?"

Mallory used the draw sheet to reposition him for his morning care. She'd have him squeaky clean in no time and ready for range-of-motion exercises. Did he have a choice? No.

Somewhere, halfway through his exercises, she got the idea to get him out of bed and into the bedside chair. A patient lift sat unused in the cluttered corner of the room. She rolled it to the bedside and positioned it over the bed, soon realizing she'd need Jake's assistance to get JT onto the canvas transporter.

She paged Jake, and twenty minutes later, much to JT's chagrin, the two of them had him off the bed and on a portable patient lounger, an adjustable chair similar to what was found in a dentist's office. She'd placed him in a near sitting position with the side rails locked in place and pushed him in front of the window, so he could see something besides four walls.

Mallory wiped and clapped her hands in an exaggerated manner, and smiled at her fish-out-of-water patient. He looked a bit twisted and listed to one side, but it would do.

"Now I can change your bedding without breaking my back."

"I think you already did break your back," Jake said, on his way out of the room. "I know you broke mine. That was no easy transfer."

"The lift did all of the work. All we had to do was swing him over to the chair and hoist him up a bit." And for JT's benefit, she said, "And I have attended annual ergonomics updates at work. I know exactly what to do." She raised a brow and looked over her shoulder to see if JT responded.

He coughed.

Before she'd finished putting fresh linen on

the hospital bed, Dr. Berger arrived for his daily visit. His stern look warned her he wasn't happy. He glared at her. When he turned to look at his patient, she noticed thinning brown hair.

"What in the world do you think you're doing?" He glanced down at JT and said, "I'm sorry, JT. I thought your rules were made quite clear." He looked at Mallory again. "I want him back in the bed immediately. Who gave you permission to get him up?"

"Are you sure you want to keep him bedridden? It takes three days of rehab for each day spent in a bed. At this rate, it'll take six months to have him walking again."

"He is in no condition to be up."

Knowing she'd never win this debate, she decided to change the subject while she bundled up the dirty linen and pushed it into the hamper.

"OK, as soon as I change the linen I'll put him back. Dr. Berger, speaking of his condition, what's your take on his slow improvement?"

"It's hard to say with a tricky disease like Guillain-Barré. We have to wait patiently for his immune system to quit attacking his nervous system."

"Did he undergo plasmaphoresis therapy or high-dose immunoglobulin treatment in the beginning?"

"We did what we could. We concentrated on stabilizing care—fluids, ventilation, and sedation. I suggest you leave the doctoring to me, and I'll leave the nursing to you." He gave a stern and condescending glance her way. "Though with JT out of bed under these conditions, I'm in serious doubt of both your qualifications and assessment skills. There's no one here to help you if he goes down."

JT coughed against the ventilator pressure and set off an alarm.

Shocked by the resistance she'd come up against with Dr. Berger, she glanced at JT. He looked helpless and cockeyed belted in the chair, yet he managed a pleasant enough look for both Mallory and Dr. Berger. He must be comfortable, but how could he tell, being paralyzed? Had she made a bad decision by getting him out of bed?

JT seemed to be trying to communicate something to her with his expression. Something she couldn't quite make out. She followed the direction of his eyes and saw it—his catheter bag had fallen to the floor. So he was completely aware of his surroundings. She quickly stooped down and hung it on the side of the chair before Dr. Berger could find one more thing to nit-pick about.

After glancing at the chart, Dr. Berger felt JT's wrist to check his pulse. He listened briefly to his lungs, though Mallory couldn't tell for sure who breathed louder, Dr. Berger or the ventilator. He looked into JT's eyes as though no one was home, and asked Mallory what his latest blood-pressure reading had been. He hadn't even realized that JT had recovered the ability to move his face. He turned and scribbled a few sentences into his chart. JT crossed his eyes at him when his back was turned.

Mallory sputtered a laugh and quickly covered her mouth, pretending to sneeze.

"I want him put back into the bed, now," Dr Berger said in a patronizing voice as he prepared to leave. "JT." He patted his patient benignly on the shoulder. "We're doing everything we can for you. Hang on. This will all work out. In the meantime, I'm covering for you as Medical Director. I'm doing the best I can, though I know it's hard to fill your shoes." Dr. Berger made a pitiful attempt at a smile for JT then repeated a curt warning growl to Mallory. "Get him back to bed. And if you're sneezing, wear a mask."

Once the door had closed, Mallory said, "Yes, sir. Right away, sir…" And saluted. She winked at JT with no intention of putting him back to bed for another hour. J.T. winked back. Delighted to see his response, she grinned. "We'll show him," she whispered into his ear, after the doctor was well out of hearing range.

She shouldn't have gotten so close to him. It took everything in her power not to peck him on the cheek. She knew her care to JT went beyond her nursing role, and her personal feelings blurred the line. She longed to caress his cheek with her hand and gaze into his eyes and tell him how she really felt. But he was her patient.

For the first time that morning JT smiled, and Mallory felt honored to be the one he'd shared it with.

Over the next three weekends Mallory developed a routine with JT. She made a point of primping and fixing up a bit, trying to look her best. She'd even experimented with wearing her hair differently than the usual single French braid down her back. She knew it was nothing more than shameless vanity, yet she did it every time she worked with him. Who was she trying to impress? Surely he never noticed.

She'd bring new music—Gershwin, Scott Joplin, Debussy, and even a little Van Morrison—get him up in the chair, do his exercises after his bath and talk to him non-stop. Anything on her mind she'd share with him. Last weekend she'd told him all about her daughter—how bright she was, where she intended to go to school, and confessed how hard it would be to live all alone again. A part of her felt like she was rebuilding their old friendship. Another part simply loved being close to him.

Being unable to speak himself, he was the perfect audience. And as he never rolled his eyes or gave her any indication that she was trying his nerves, she kept up her monologues, keeping him connected with the world and up to date on her rather mundane personal life.

During lunch, she'd read him the sports page, something she'd never do on her own, but as he'd perk up and look mildly interested, she made it a part of their routine. After his dinner she'd read from the Arthur Rimbaud book, and found herself growing fascinated with the young and decidedly mad poet.

She'd end her shift by tucking him into bed while playing piano sonatas on the CD. When she left each Saturday and Sunday night, she knew she'd tried her best and given him her all.

He always looked peaceful when he slept— thick black lashes resting on his high cheek-bones—like a child. She longed to run her thumb over them for an excuse to touch him one more time before she left for home. But she knew that would be highly unprofessional and way out of bounds of their patient-nurse relationship.

* * *

The next Saturday morning, looking forward to seeing him after a long week at Mercy Hospital, she had a surprise when she parked her car. A respiratory care truck was in the driveway, loading the ventilator into the back.

"Did he get a new one?" she asked.

"Nah. He won't be needing it any more."

Her heart sank. Oh, God. No one had called her to say Dr. Prescott had died. Tears sprang to her eyes, and stung. Water formed in her mouth and she thought she might throw up. Oh, God. What had gone wrong? He had been doing so well last weekend.

She ran past the men loading the ventilator and into the house to his first-story bedroom. The night nurse was nowhere to be found. She took a deep breath and pushed through the door, prepared to see JT dead.

He lay perfectly still, peaceful and silent. She bit her lower lip and whimpered. Tears blurred her vision. She used the cuff of her hand to push the tears out of the way, and walked closer to his bed. Her stomach tightened into a knot and it became hard to breathe. He must have just died.

The IV was still infusing, and they hadn't removed the catheter bag yet.

With a shaky hand she smoothed her hair and tried to regain her composure before the other nurse returned and saw her blubbering. She noticed his trach had been capped off and decided to lean over and examine him up close, one last time.

One big blue eye popped open. "Good morning, sunshine," he said in a weak raspy voice.

She jumped back and screamed. "You're alive!" Wildly relieved yet flustered by his trick, she fought her smile and offered a scolding look. "Do you have any idea what I thought when I saw them rolling the ventilator onto the truck?"

"That Jake had pulled the plug on me?"

She screwed up her face and tossed her head. "What a ridiculous notion. Who'd ever think up anything like that?"

He crooked his mouth into a smirk. "Some control freak idiot?"

She stood perfectly still for a moment, deciding whether or not to take him seriously.

She saw the twinkle in his eyes and played along. "Why, Dr Prescott, I had no idea you had a sense of humor."

"I don't."

They stared at each other for another second before they broke into a laugh. Well, she did anyway. His was more like an air laugh, he made the gestures but nothing came out of his mouth.

"I'm so glad to see you alive and talking, I could kiss you."

He cleared his throat. "I wish you would."

Their playful moment suddenly grew serious. She stared into his face, assessing whether he'd meant what he'd just said or had simply been teasing her. She couldn't hide the fact from herself that she would like to kiss him, but would never allow herself to on the job or, heaven forbid, ever let him know she'd like to.

Mallory smoothed her nurse's uniform and swallowed a lump in her throat. She nervously fiddled with her hair and said, "I'll get things started for your bath."

Seeing a different side of JT had shaken her to the core. She retreated to the basin in the bathroom, business as usual. When he'd been unable to respond, he'd seemed safe. Yet now, discovering he'd been thinking things all along and could only just now begin to express himself, she realized their relationship had changed. And it scared her.

"That's not fair, you know," he called out in a brittle voice.

"What's not fair?"

"You get to see me naked, but I never get to see you in the buff."

She almost spilled the water from the bowl and felt a blush so deep she knew her face had turned scarlet. How could she face him after that?

But this was her *job* and she would work to the best of her ability for her *patient,* she reminded herself as she pushed the tempting thought of being naked with J.T. Prescott far into the back of her mind.

Later, after the most awkward bed bath so far, as was their routine, she did range-of-motion exercises, starting with his feet and ending with his arms. She made the final stretch with extra vigor and leaned over him, pushing his arm far above his head.

"Not that I'm complaining or anything, but your breast always hits me in the face when we do this one."

She dropped his arm and backed off in horror.

"I could never tell you before." He smirked and winked. "But it's definitely my favorite exercise."

Realizing how true his statement was, she cringed. For the second time that day she blushed.

How intimate they'd become—forehead to forehead, their breath mingling, skin touching skin while she stretched and worked his joints, tendons, and muscles. She couldn't bear the closeness another second and turned to something safe, business as usual.

"I think you should know that I've committed a patient confidentiality violation with you."

"How novel, a nurse reading her patient's chart. Yes, you've definitely invaded my privacy. So what sign am I?"

"What?"

"Leo? Or Cancer?"

She shook her head in exasperation, thinking how much more like his old self he seemed. "Leo. No, what I'm trying to say is I checked out your hospital chart and discovered they never even tried plasmaphoresis. I've read in one of your medical books that it could reduce the severity and duration of the GBS episode."

His joking eyes turned serious. "What did they do for me?"

"They gave you high-dose immunoglobulins and steroids."

They stared at each other for a long, steady moment.

"I'm sure there's a reason. I'll ask Wayne Berger tomorrow."

"But you can't let him know I read your hospital chart. I could get fired."

"I won't let you get fired. Listen, it's all touch and go with treating a crazy disease like this. Because something works one time, it doesn't necessarily mean it will work for me. I'm sure there is a logical reason why Wayne didn't try the best method of reducing the severity and duration of GBS."

Suddenly seeming very agitated, JT squinted

and turned away. "Damn. He used steroid hormones? That can have a deleterious effect on GBS. I'm going to demand to know my course of treatment, and I'll keep you informed."

"Maybe you should ask for plasmaphoresis."

"It's a thought. I need some time to digest this information, Mallory."

Her eyes drifted to his arm, the one she'd just been stretching, and it occurred to her that it hadn't flopped like dead weight when she'd dropped it earlier. She switched to the other side of his body, and though the exercise worked more awkwardly with her avoiding smashing her breast in his face, she gave him her best stretch effort.

"Now I'm definitely disappointed," he said.

"About what?"

"You've moved your chest away."

"Oh, stop it." She tapped his shoulder with her middle finger.

"And I've been thinking about something else, too."

"What's that?"

"As you know all this information about me, it's

only fair that you should share something private with me. Something I'd never find out on my own."

She took a deep breath. So he wanted to balance the scales. What in the world could she expose about herself to JT? She thought for a moment, cleared her throat and blurted, "I got pregnant on my prom night."

"Must have been some party."

"Hardly. The whole thing was very disappointing."

"Why is it you've never gotten married?"

She hesitated. Would she come off as pitiful if she told him the truth? Well, she'd told him about getting pregnant, so she may as well come clean on this too. "No one has ever asked."

His eyes softened when he looked at her. She felt exposed, yet not embarrassed. Somehow it felt OK for JT to know that she'd never been proposed to.

He didn't break eye contact. She had the strange sensation that he wanted to run his hand through her hair. She'd only pulled it half up today, and several long tendrils hung over her shoulders.

"Sometimes I think the world is filled with stupid men," he said.

Though touched by his comment, she decided to keep the moment light. "Did you by any chance include yourself in that? I'm still put out that you never hinted about my breast in your face before today."

"I may be paralyzed, but I'm still a man. I didn't want to ruin a good thing. It's been quite enjoyable all along." He grinned.

"You're horrible!" She finished stretching his arm, and brought it back to his side. Desperately trying to keep the upper hand in a situation quickly spinning out of her control, she pinched his cheek and smiled.

Mallory felt a pinch on her thigh, high up, almost on her bottom. She jumped, and realized what had happened. "You've got strength back in your arms?"

He imitated lobster claws with his hands.

"I could scream," she said, excitement bubbling up inside her chest.

"Oh, please, don't do that, again. Better yet, kiss me like you said before."

She studied his eyes to see if he was serious. He had apparently turned into a jokester since he'd gotten off the vent. After exchanging a long searching stare, each measuring the other's level of seriousness and afraid to cross the patient-nurse barrier, she lifted his hand and gave a motherly peck to his knuckles.

He returned a decidedly disappointed look that said, That's not good enough.

CHAPTER FOUR

MALLORY tossed and turned all night. Visions of her imaginary passionate kiss with JT kept forcing their way into her mind, and she couldn't go to sleep. Having only brushed his knuckles with her lips in reality, in fantasy she'd met his mouth with her own and given him a long and deep kiss—the kind of kiss that was an invitation to much, much more.

She'd hardly been able to face him the rest of the day, wanting desperately to kiss him!

After an intense cringe, she flopped onto her back and ran her fingers through her hair. "Ugh." She had to keep this job professional. Then another thought popped into her mind.

Travel shots! If JT had planned a trip to Kenya, he'd have had to get specific travel shots a few weeks prior to leaving the country. Could one of those inoculations have caused his GBS? She made a mental note to track down the shot clinic nurse at work then rolled back onto her stomach and planned how she'd behave like the perfect lady tomorrow, so he'd never suspect how much she was attracted to him.

Mallory arrived at JT's on Sunday morning looking fresh and bubbling with life. She also evaded making eye contact with him. Hmm. Maybe he'd pushed it too far yesterday. Maybe he'd misread her cues. They'd always gotten along so easily at Mercy Hospital, and they'd been through so much together recently that he'd forgotten this was only her job. He promised to be on good behavior today, though it would be hard, considering how she'd stirred him up.

JT took a deep breath and tried to think of something non-threatening to say to his special nurse.

Before he had a chance, like a bad dream, his ex-wife stuck her face inside the door, distracting him, just as Mallory slipped into the bathroom to fill his bed-bath basin. Looking aloof and perfectly made up as usual—her hair colored golden with no sign of dark roots, a bit longer than her usual below-the-jaw cut—he wondered how Samantha had gotten into the house.

"James?"

"Samantha," he said, forcing a neutral tone, knowing his blood pressure would probably register twenty points higher if taken now.

"I've brought Corey, like we discussed on the phone."

The day, once again, looked promising and he felt his blood pressure even out. Finally, a visit from the one person he loved more than life itself. His son peered around the corner of the door, like a shy stranger. His own son. Was he afraid of him?

Samantha had elected to keep him away for all these weeks so as not to traumatize him. Now that he could talk, JT had put his foot down and insisted that she bring his son for the court-ordered visits. He wouldn't let her get away with keeping Corey all to herself any longer.

"Come here, Corey. I won't bite."

"Aren't you sick?"

"Yes, but I'm not contagious, bud." He raised his right hand. "I promise." He wondered why Samantha hadn't explained that to their son yet.

Corey had filled out more. He seemed taller, too. Trying to act older than his ten years, he'd started combing his hair upward in a *faux* Mohawk, reminding JT more of a little rascal than a cool pre-teen. He smiled, and Corey cautiously stepped up to the bed.

"Let me see how much you've grown." Up close, he realized Samantha had let Corey get his ear pierced without consulting him first. What indulgence would she allow next, a brow piercing at twelve, a tattoo at fourteen?

He clenched his jaw and tried to keep positive. "So how's school going?"

Corey shrugged. "I dunno."

A painfully awkward fifteen minutes followed. Mallory wisely stayed out of sight. Samantha was only doing her duty to appease the lawyers. He knew she thought she had the upper hand, with him being bedridden, but he still intended to demand the every-other-weekend visitation rights he'd fought for in court.

Just when she'd made a move to pick up her purse to leave, Mallory appeared like a sorceress and a blue rubber ball whizzed past Samantha's head toward Corey.

"Think fast!" Mallory said, her smile cheeky.

Corey caught the ball with one hand, looking startled but pleased.

"And again!" She tossed another.

He deftly caught that one, too. And for the first time during their visit he smiled.

"Hi." She nodded to a surprised-looking Samantha. "I'm Nurse Glenn." She turned her attention immediately to Corey.

"Those are exercise balls. Let me show you how your dad uses them."

She took one of the balls and held it in the palm of her hand and squeezed. "Like this. See?" She helped Corey place it in JT's hand and squeeze it with him. "That's right. We're trying to help him get his strength back. Before you know it, he'll be walking again."

Corey relaxed with a specific job to do. He smiled up at JT and asked. "Do you feel stronger, Dad?"

JT grinned. "Yeah. I do." Without giving it a thought he tossed the ball to Corey, who tossed it back, quickly digressing from the strengthening exercise to an even better test of reflexes. "I couldn't do that last week." He dropped the first return ball and then the other when Corey threw them back at him. He chuckled, and Corey joined him. "I guess I still can't."

"You did good for a while, Dad."

He rubbed the top of his son's head. "Thanks. What's this style called?"

"Aw, it's nothin'. Mom said I should try it." He smoothed it forward, fixing his hair back to the usual way he'd worn it.

"I hate to break things up, but he's got a soccer game at ten-thirty," came Samantha's cold drone.

Corey glanced at him like he was torn about leaving so soon. JT didn't want to cause him any unnecessary concern. He was damned if he'd lay any guilt on his kid.

"Hey, you kick that ball around for your old man today, OK?"

"I'll score a goal for you." His face lit up, and he stood on his toes to reach over the big hospital bed and hug JT goodbye. Neither let go for a couple of seconds. It felt too good. JT sensed that Corey needed the hug as much as he did. His son meant the world to him, and having him in his arms was the biggest boost to his spirits since the overly chatty yet peculiarly appealing Mallory Glenn had shown up in his life.

"Call me tonight and let me know how you did."

"OK."

When Samantha steered Corey out the door, JT spoke up. "I'd like him to stay with me all day next Saturday."

"He's got two soccer games next Saturday."

"Then Sunday. Bring him over for a few hours on Sunday."

"We'll see," she said as she shut the door.

JT threw the ball and hit the wall.

Mallory had the good sense to stay quiet. If she'd said anything just then, he'd have brushed her off. Maybe even growled. Feeling out of control and helpless drove him nuts. His son was slipping through his fingers, and there was nothing he could do about it. He needed to get well, and soon.

* * *

Something told her to stay out of JT's way for a while after Corey left. He was a beautiful, healthy-looking kid, strongly resembling his father with deep blue eyes and a winning smile. The huge dimples he'd inherited from his mother. How hard it must be for JT not to see his son daily. As a mother, she knew it would rip her heart out.

Samantha Prescott was nothing short of drop-dead gorgeous. Tall, shapely, and impeccably dressed, she was a real high-class soccer mom. How could she come close to measuring up to her? She must have been out of her mind to fantasize about JT yesterday. As if anything could ever happen.

Had he spent enough time stewing over his son? She was about to find out as it was time to change the dressing and clean around his subclavian line.

She flicked his arm with her finger. "Quit sulking. It's not becoming."

He stared straight ahead then glanced at her. The sparkle in his eyes had changed to dull sadness. "She wants full custody of Corey. I told her over my dead body." He shook his head and gave a quick laugh. "She almost got her wish. My illness is giving her the upper hand, and it's killing me."

He leaned back on his pillow and dug his fingers into his hair. He stared at the ceiling for several seconds, his jaw muscles clenching. "I can't ever let that happen."

Not on my shift, it won't, she thought.

Mallory bit her nail while deep in thought. The dim lamp cast eerie shadows across the walls of JT's room. She sat in the leather chair, feet propped casually on the ottoman.

The hospital bed was in the high position, allowing JT to read the newspaper under a bedside gooseneck lamp. His mood had lifted after Corey called to report he'd scored not one but two goals for his father at the soccer game.

Her brain whirled, and the silence in the room nearly drove her crazy. She couldn't keep her mouth shut another second.

"So, what shots did you need to get when you were preparing for your trip?" she blurted out.

"Hmm?" He raised his head, his thick black hair kissing his shoulders, a day's growth of beard shadowing his cheeks. He'd protested when she'd tried to shave him that morning after his son had left.

"Your travel shots. What were they?"

He furrowed his brow and drew in his chin, eyes cast upward in thought. "Let's see. Yellow fever. Tetanus and diphtheria. Typhoid. Polio and hepatitis A. Oh, and some pills for malaria."

"Have any of those shots been reported to the centers for disease control as causing GBS?"

He shook his head and looked dully at her. "Haven't a clue."

"Well, think about it. It's important." It came out more gruffly than she'd meant. She'd only said it because she cared, but what must he think of his nurse talking to him like that?

An amused look crossed his face. He smirked. "I kind of like it when you talk tough."

She huffed and rolled her eyes. "Did you ask Dr. Berger why he didn't try plasmaphoresis immediately on you?"

"As a matter of fact, I did. He said I had an

unstable heart rate the first couple of days. He opted to try the immunoglobulins instead."

"A lot of good that did you."

"It's all a crapshoot anyway, Mallory. GBS has no cure. It isn't always controllable either."

"Has your spinal fluid changed?"

"I'm not letting him tap me again, if that's what you're asking."

"But why not try the plasmaphoresis? It could get rid of the rest of the toxic antibodies."

"Have you seen the size of the needles they use for that?"

"Come on, JT." She stopped cold. She'd used his name. It had been the first time. Sure, she'd thought it a million times, always used it when she imagined them wrapped in each other's arms, but to actually say it out loud?

A curious smile spread across his face. "Are you working at the hospital tomorrow?" he asked.

"Not until Tuesday."

"Listen, when you work on Tuesday, go to my office." He pointed to his dresser. "My office keys should be in that ceramic bowl with all the change."

She stood and crossed the room to dig through the change. The keys were attached to a leather lanyard that looked as if it had been braided by a young boy. No doubt Corey had made it at summer camp or craft day at school. She held it up. A man who could afford sterling silver or gold carried a simple keyring made by his son. The thought touched her deeply.

"There you go," he said. "Go to my office and you'll find the latest Center for Disease Control report on my desk. Maybe something will be there."

"That's great. Shall I bring it with me next Saturday?"

His eyes studied hers for a moment, then drifted away in thought. "Actually, I was hoping you'd bring them by on Tuesday night. That is, if you don't have any plans. Now that Wayne's letting me have thick liquids, I'd love to have a smoothie, too." He smiled like a little boy. "You know, something with a protein or vitamin boost or whatever."

What could she say?

"I don't have plans. What flavor?"

"Peach."

"Will do. Tuesday night it is then."

Mallory felt like a thief in the night, letting herself into Dr. Prescott's office on Tuesday after her shift. Surprised by the ease with which she found the CDC reports, she gathered them up and swept out of the room almost as quickly as she'd entered.

Once home, she took great care to choose a pair of slacks that fit to her advantage and a colorful form-hugging blouse that brought out the green flecks in her hazel eyes. She left her hair down and brushed it to smooth it out and make it shine. It reached her lower back. She applied mascara, lipstick and gloss, and pinched her cheeks to pink them up. She'd given up on trying to cover her freckles with make-up or powder.

Finally, she felt ready to leave her condo to buy JT's peach smoothie and venture back to his house.

Was this a date? Not likely. She chided herself about making a big deal out of him asking her over. Still, the atmosphere would be completely different tonight.

Mallory arrived at the cozy Spanish-styled home in the Los Feliz Hills a few minutes before eight. To give herself time to gather her thoughts, she paused inside the car to enjoy the sparkling night-time view of Los Angeles. She parked in the driveway and walked under the large cocoa-brown stucco arch to reach his front door. The evening was warm and dry. Potent night-blooming jasmine bushes lining the walkway tickled her nose with their scent. Using the brass knocker, she tapped out a friendly rhythm, leaving the last two beats hanging.

The house she visited each weekend seemed so different when she came as a friend instead of a nurse. Her stomach tightened a bit.

The weeknight nurse opened the door, looking puzzled. As Mallory only worked the weekends, they'd never met.

"Hello," Mallory said. "I'm here to visit Dr. Prescott."

"Oh. Let me check if he wants company." She closed the heavy rustic wood door in Mallory's face.

A few seconds later, she reopened the door

with a smile. "Come on in. The doctor is waiting," she said with a sweeping gesture, giggling at her silly joke.

When Mallory reached JT's room, she became breathless. Someone had sent a barber since Sunday. He looked clean-cut and dashing, with a sparkle in his eyes. They'd removed the tracheostomy, and a small gauze dressing covered the wound.

"She's my friend," he said in a voice stronger than she'd remembered from last Sunday, and gestured toward Mallory. "We'll be fine. You can take a break."

He looked beyond pleased to see her. If she read his expression correctly, he was taken with her choice of outfit.

She offered the smoothie from behind her back as if a surprise gift. His eyebrows shot up in delight.

"You shouldn't have," he said, when he took it.

"You told me to."

"Ah. I did, didn't I?" He took a sip through the large straw. "Heaven. Pure and simple." He lifted an ever- strengthening arm in a Shakespearian actor's pose. "How does man survive when fed through a stomach tube alone?"

She giggled. "I don't know. You're the thespian, do tell."

He deadpanned. "It was a rhetorical question." He gave her a feigned impatient look and sipped more. Taking her cue, he continued, "But since you've asked…" He dramatically raised his arm again. "It's only half a life when you can't taste or eat. Like eating fettuccine without Alfredo or marinara sauce."

He slurped his drink with great flourish and she smiled at his obvious joy.

Mallory didn't move when his attention turned from the smoothie to her. He rolled his eyes from the tip of her head down to her rhinestone-trimmed sandals, and suddenly she was glad she'd worn them and almost wiggled her toes so he'd notice her ruby-red toenails.

JT grew serious, his gaze intent on her, his voice close to a whisper. "One last comparison, if I may? It's like seeing Mallory in a nursing uniform when she could be wearing her black slacks and sexy blouse every day." He whistled through his teeth. "You are off duty, right?"

She nodded and smiled, enjoying a subtle chill across her shoulders.

He grinned. Deep lines, like parentheses, formed around his mouth. He lowered his voice. "Lady, you look hot."

Heat rose to her face. She willed it down and nervously scooped and swept her hair over her shoulder to cover her cleavage, realizing he probably thought she was posing for him instead. She dug into her shoulder-bag and produced the CDC reports he'd asked her to bring, preferring to stick to business as usual than explore this newfound electricity between them. Though her mouth had gone dry, she managed to say, "Thank you."

He patted beside him. "Come. Sit." She did. He gestured for her to move closer.

She'd never given his bed a second thought when she'd reported to work. But now, off duty, it took on a whole new meaning. She moved closer and sat gingerly beside him.

Her non-official bed-sitting seemed awkward,

and she tensed up. That was until she looked into his eyes. They shone dark blue, like lapis lazuli, and she felt drawn into their special hue. Drawn toward the man that possessed them.

He smiled softly at her, she moved closer, and his arm slipped around her shoulders. "That's better," he said. They snuggled close to share the overhead lamp, and together they studied the CDC report, while she tried unsuccessfully not to develop goose-bumps.

No great discovery followed. Then a light appeared in his eyes.

"We should be reading the World Health Organization reports, not these. Now I remember. Kenya had an outbreak of meningitis a couple of years ago, and the travel clinic recommended getting a shot for it."

"So you think it could be the meningitis shot that set you off?"

"It's possible. It takes four weeks to develop a fourfold immune response, and that's right about the time I got sick."

"We need to report this, in case there is a pattern that can be stopped."

"That's a good point," he said.

"We also need to think how this knowledge can help you now."

"Maybe it's time for a plasma exchange."

"Well." She clapped her hands together. "There's no time like the present."

Mallory shifted on the bed in order to look at him better. He took her hands in his and squeezed them. She could feel new strength in his grasp.

"Thank you for caring about me," he whispered, sincerity softening his eyes. "In all this mess, I feel like you're the only one on my side."

She smiled, basking in the pleasure of his gaze. He made her feel special, as if only she had the answers. As if he knew how much she felt for him. A sudden blaze sprang to her cheeks.

"And if memory serves me right," he said, with one raised brow and a gleam in his eyes, "you *are* off duty."

She nodded, feeling suddenly schoolgirl-shy.

"Have I ever told you how your beautiful eyes helped ground me? And did you know you have tiny green and gold flecks in them?"

She shook her head, mesmerized by his words.

"I was panicking about being trapped inside my body, and there you were, confident and gentle. You helped me remember I was still a man." His hand gently threaded through her hair.

His face grew blurred as involuntary tingles started behind her eyelids. She blinked to bring him back into focus.

"I knew when you were here with me, I was safe. Someone would fight *for* me—even if it meant fighting *me*. I knew you gave a damn."

Enthralled by his gaze, she swallowed a swell of emotion and subtly moistened her lips.

Steady hands guided her face to his. Looking her soundly in the eyes, he placed a long, luscious kiss on her lips.

Instantly, something broke free between them. Their mouths and tongues mingled, almost frantic to connect. His warm and deep explorations sent a shiver through her. She welcomed his tongue. He tasted sweet, like peaches.

Knowing he'd recovered sensitivity in his face, neck and shoulders, she concentrated on those parts of his body. She pressed his shoulders flush to the elevated bed and pillow and kissed him back. She licked the side of his neck and tugged on his earlobe with her teeth. He'd obviously spruced up for her, tasting clean and smelling of citrus aftershave.

He groaned in a satisfying response.

"You started it," she whispered.

He touched her lips with his own, talking over them. "And I'm so glad I did."

Before kissing him the way she really wanted to, her eyes drifted to the video camera in the corner of the room. "What about that?"

"I had Jake shut it down the minute I could talk again." His strengthening hands guided her back to him. "I've got my voice back, I don't need video protection."

"Maybe it's time to have him remove it altogether," she said.

His finger traced her jaw before he held her chin. Staring intently at her, he said, "I promise I won't tell if you take advantage of me." Heat flashed in his eyes. He drew her mouth to his and kissed her as if he hadn't kissed anyone in years.

She moaned a resoundingly grateful response.

Mallory heard footsteps in the hall and quickly broke off the kiss. Frantic to look as if nothing had happened—as though the most spectacular kiss of her life hadn't knocked her sandals off— she stood, ran her hands over her hair and stepped back. Embarrassed, she didn't make eye contact with JT.

The nurse tapped on the door and stuck her head inside the room. "Need anything?"

"I'm fine, Gloria, thanks." His voice didn't betray an ounce of emotion. Back to business as usual.

The second the door shut, his hand shot out and grasped her wrist, pulling her back toward him. Fire traveled up her arm and fanned across her chest. Her breathing became shallow and quick.

Confusion, fear, and a deep sense of duty had her reaching for the smoothie on the bedside table and shoving it between them.

"Here," she said.

Disappointment showed in his eyes.

"It doesn't feel right," she continued. "You know? I'm your nurse."

"Not tonight you aren't." He put the smoothie back on the table. "I asked you here as my friend, and I discovered what I'd suspected all along." His hand swept back her hair from her face, and his fingers played with the ends, examining it as if a treasure. "I hate waiting five days to see you every week. You've changed my life and the way I look at things. You've helped me give up my over-serious attitude and lighten up."

Unable to resist, she ran her fingertips across his cheek. "I think your illness may have done that."

He pressed into her hand. "That, too. But you…" He shook his head, his eyes sparkling with wonderment. "You are the most glorious discovery I have made in a long, long time." His hands massaged her shoulders, kneading and drawing her closer. They ran down her arms until he took her hands in his. "I'm forty years old, I've traveled the world and accomplished a great deal, but I've never found anyone quite like you…until now."

Afraid to leap at a chance to explore a new and exciting relationship with a man who happened to be her patient, Mallory felt confused and insecure. She stiffened and tried to figure out the best way to word what she needed to say.

"You know, JT, sometimes patients get gratitude mixed up with desire."

"You don't think a man can fall for you on your own gorgeous merits? You think that my attraction has got to be gratitude, as you put it?"

"Surely in your practice you've had women fall for you, and you knew it was simply because you had helped them."

"Of course, every doctor has experienced that. That's why I'm the perfect judge to figure out that this 'thing' between us is completely different. Honey, if you can't tell sexual attraction from gratitude, you need to go back and repeat your courses on human sexuality."

Mallory giggled, and lightened up on her self-doubt.

"But if you're not interested…"

"Oh, no, it's not that," she replied quickly.

They stared at each other in silence for several seconds. Her hands trembled gently in his grasp as the impact of what he'd just told her and what she'd just admitted sank in. He helped her steady her hands.

"Let me look at you." He gazed at her as though she were something sacred. "I want to remember how beautiful you look tonight." He quickly kissed her knuckles as though having just made a snap decision. "In fact, hand me my camera. I want to take your picture."

"No!" she said on a burst of embarrassment. "Oh, God, no."

"I don't know if I can do you justice, but I'd like to try to capture your exquisite face. The way your eyes smile even when you're trying to be serious. How your nose crinkles when you can't believe something—like right now." He smiled and reached out to feel the ends of her hair, examining them reverently. "I'd love to capture the most beautiful shade of red I've ever seen." He slowly twined the hair around his fingers and gently drew her closer to kiss the tip of her nose. He teased her lips with his, speaking softly. "Let me take your picture. Please."

Mallory took a deep breath—how could she refuse him? After another insanely wonderful kiss she walked to his dresser to get the camera. She handed it to him, and he took it in silence.

"Now, sit over there." He used two fingers to gesture toward the chair.

She sat awkwardly, as if she were a child on picture day at school.

"Relax, sunshine," he soothed, looking through the viewer and adjusting the settings and lens.

Slowly, with sweet and comforting words, he coaxed her to settle down and feel natural. He asked her questions about herself and snapped pictures when she answered. A million thoughts swirled through her mind. What was she doing there? Why had she let herself become emotionally involved with a patient? He clicked another picture. Oh, what the hell. She vamped and slid her blouse off her shoulder just a tad. He snapped again. She crossed her eyes and stuck out her tongue. He took another shot. She gave him an exasperated look, and he snapped again. Frustrated, she dug her hands into her hair and gave a mock scream—and he took yet another picture.

The scream brought the nurse rushing back into the room. Suddenly remembering they weren't alone, Mallory stood, feeling guilty for disturbing the peace.

"We were just horsing around with the camera. Sorry. I guess it's time to go," she said.

Disappointment covered his face but something flashed in his gaze. "Friday night. Chinese," he said.

She rolled her eyes and shook her head. "You're not eating solids yet."

"But you are. You told me you liked Chinese food. Come back and visit Friday night."

JT would count the minutes until Friday when Mallory returned. She'd become the rainbow in his dead world, and he loved each second with her. He'd quit caring about anyone except his son until Mallory had walked into his life. And he was crazy about her. How could she interpret what he felt for her as gratitude? Oh, no. These feelings went much deeper.

He'd realized that the GBS had receded even more when they'd kissed, by the reaction below his waist. And now his emotional paralysis was receding as well. He had something to live for, and he wanted to get well.

He picked up the phone and dialed. He would call Wayne Berger and demand plasmaphoresis a.s.a.p. He wanted his life back, and he wanted it back now. And if exchanging his plasma with washed cells meant the GBS might recede completely so he could walk again, he'd do it.

Playing the victim had never, ever suited him.

Mallory worked diligently with a post-op patient on Wednesday. She checked the vital signs every fifteen minutes, and lifted the blanket to examine the dressing for any excessive bleeding. She assessed the patient's pain level. Emptied the drain and recorded the serosanguinous fluid, along with the secretions from the nasogastric tube in the Gomco machine, and wrote them both on the intake and output sheet.

Yet every waking moment since their kiss last night she'd thought about JT. He'd rocked her to her toes and she was almost certain she'd done the same to him—that was, if he could feel his toes. Bad joke, she knew, but how else was she supposed to handle their circumstances?

He was her patient. His illness had brought them together. He'd never have given her the time of day otherwise. Oh, she'd read plenty of those sappy opposites-stranded-on-an-island-together novels. Things always worked out happily ever after for them, but in reality? She'd always wondered how the story would end if the author picked it up a few months down the road, back in the real world, where the grunting peon didn't fit in with the socialite's friends, or vice versa.

Sure, he'd said a bunch of pretty words to her before they'd kissed. But maybe he'd thought he'd had to. No one had to remind her she was nothing more than a distraction to JT while he recovered.

But there simply was no way to ignore the kiss that had opened up her fantasy world, this time larger than life, in living color! And JT was the star.

As far as she was concerned, he'd asked her out on another date for Friday night, and she planned to enjoy every minute of it. And if she was lucky, he'd kiss her again.

She asked the nurse's aide to empty the catheter bag while she went to get a pain shot for the post-op patient. Before she reached the med room, the ward clerk called out her name.

"You've got a call. Dr. Prescott wants to talk to you."

Dr. Prescott? Calling her at work? Maybe he'd thought of something else he wanted her to bring home from his office.

"This is Mallory."

"Hey, sunshine. Listen, I need some moral support. Can you come to the dialysis unit? I'm about to get stuck with a needle the size of the Holland tunnel."

"You're having plasmaphoresis?"

"Will you come and hold my hand, Nurse Glenn?"

"I'll see if I can take an early lunch. Let me give this shot first. OK?"

"I'll be waiting."

Holy cow. He'd called her at work as if he were her boyfriend. He wanted to see her, too.

Yeah, but that could just be out of friendship and fear of needles. But he'd called her "sunshine," the nickname he'd given her. This "thing" between them was definitely more than friendship.

Her pulse did a little dance, and her face grew warm. Nothing would stop her from holding JT's hand.

JT watched the nurse assemble her intravenous equipment after she'd stuck on the heart-monitor leads to his chest and applied the automatic blood-pressure cuff to his arm. He'd been brought to the hospital in an ambulance ordered by Wayne Berger. Now he reclined on the lounge chair in the dialysis unit, waiting for the treatment to start.

Secluded in his little world for so long, he'd forgotten how good it felt to be out among the living again. He loved medicine, and missed practicing it. Odd, when he'd opted to become hospital medical director, he'd given up his patient load, yet patient contact was what he had always liked the most about medicine.

Thinking back, it had been Samantha who'd encouraged him to take the job. She'd liked the prestige, the fact that he would be a mentor to all the other doctors—not to mention the pay raise. He hadn't been particularly happy since the switch in jobs, and now, if he was honest with himself, he realized he'd loathed the amount of meetings he'd had to attend and the paperwork he'd constantly had to keep up with.

Maybe he would let Wayne Berger keep his job, and he'd go back to doing what he had trained to do, practice medicine.

Mallory rushed into the dialysis unit with a smile like the first ray of light after a storm. Suddenly, for JT, all was right with the world.

"This is so exciting," she said, squeezing his hand.

The dialysis nurse raised a brow and swabbed the antecubital fossa of his right arm with an iodophor solution to disinfect his skin.

"That's easy for you to say," he said with a grimace when he glanced the size of the needle the nurse intended to stick into his vein. "Catch me if I black out."

"Quit watching," she scolded, and used her hands on his cheeks to force his head in her direction. "You'll just make it worse."

Her grasp was so tight, his lips felt puckered up. "OK. OK. Let go."

She laughed and eased up her grip.

"You'll feel a pinch," the nurse said.

"Ouch!" He jumped.

Mallory patted his hand. "It's all over now."

"That pinch felt more like a gunshot wound."

"You are such a wimp," Mallory said, and tapped his forehead with her middle finger.

"I'm not used to being on the receiving end, that's all."

"Welcome to the patients' world."

The dialysis nurse lifted her head just long enough to raise another brow before she went back to releasing the tourniquet and securing the IV catheter with a transparent dressing.

"So, tell me how this works," Mallory said to distract him further.

"The blood goes through the tubing into that centrifuge and gets separated. The plasma is removed and replaced with frozen plasma or some other substitute if there is a shortage. It gets sent back into my body all fresh and clean of the immune complexes that have been attacking my nervous system."

"Sounds like a plan. Why didn't we think of this sooner?"

"Don't get cute on me," he said, taking the obvious jab in good humor. "I invited you here for moral support, not to aggravate me."

When the dialysis nurse moved away to check on the machine, she gave them one last suspicious glance. When she was out of earshot, he leaned forward and whispered, "Though having to keep up a business façade with you is driving me insane. I'd much rather kiss you."

His words had a devastating effect on Mallory. She turned the color of her gorgeous ruby-red toenails from the night before. As if she'd realized how their relationship had changed, she removed herself from any contact with him for public scrutiny.

Damn. He'd wanted to charm her, not send her running and screaming into the sunset. But he liked the wide-eyed stare she'd cast him just now.

Her pupils were large and dark, what he liked to call bedroom eyes. He couldn't resist teasing her more.

He gave a wry smile. "If I'm lucky, in no time I'll be chasing you around the hospital bed in my room."

She said "Ah" on a quick inhalation, and her lashes fluttered. "Will you be quiet?" she whispered. "Someone might hear you."

Oh, he wanted to see that look again, but preferably when they were both naked. "Life is full of surprises, isn't it, sunshine?"

By the expression on her face, no one could have been more astonished than Mallory.

CHAPTER FIVE

MALLORY rushed out OF the dialysis unit, her face on fire. So it wasn't her imagination. She'd moved JT with her kisses. Now he wanted to take their flirting to a new level. If her memory served her correctly, she could tell he'd been somewhat aroused last night.

Oh, God, she'd behaved so unprofessionally with him. But she had been there on her day off, and he'd invited her to his home as a guest. Could she ever reconcile her misgivings about getting involved with a patient?

She hoped so, because JT was the man she'd always dreamed of—decisive, intelligent, kind, and sexy as hell, bedridden or not.

Though he was a captive audience, and she was most likely the only game in town. Her heart waved a little red flag over that bit of truth, but she ignored it. Hadn't he assured her his attraction to her wasn't out of gratitude?

If he wanted to pursue a relationship with her, she'd be there for him. After all the years of facing life alone as a mother and nurse, she owed herself a chance at romance.

Thursday, at work, Mallory sat at the bedside of a dehydrated and frail woman. She tied a tourniquet around her arm, cleaned the skin, and prepared to insert an intravenous line. Her co-worker, Jenny, had asked for her help after she'd tried twice to start the difficult IV, but had failed. The original ER admission IV had blown and left the patient's hand swollen and bruised. Mallory hated any patient to be stuck more than three times, so she knew this one chance had to be successful.

She was just about to prick the surface of the patient's skin when another nurse poked her head into the room.

"Dr. Prescott said to tell you he's waiting in the dialysis unit."

Her heart stumbled and she had to steady

her hand before she started to insert the needle into the vein.

"OK. Thanks for the info," she said, trying hard to sound blasé.

She took a cleansing breath and focused on the vein. With expert skill she managed to capture and puncture the rolling vein before it disappeared. *Violà!* The intravenous line was back in place, and Jenny's patient could get her needed fluids and antibiotics on schedule.

"I owe you one," Jenny said.

"Nah. We've got to help each other. We're a team, remember?"

Jenny took over taping the IV tubing in place. "So what's with you and Dr. Prescott? He called you yesterday, too, didn't he?"

Mallory's heart dropped. Had everyone noticed that he'd called? Should she tell the truth? Hell, no!

"I guess we've kind of become friends since I've been taking care of him on the weekends. He gets really lonely in that big old house. And you know what? I'd forgotten what a nice guy he can be, despite his gruff exterior."

Worried about what rumors might be circulating around the hospital, she decided not to rush down to visit him today, though it was the most important thing she wanted to do. Instead, she skipped lunch, did a dressing change, admitted a post-op patient to the ward, and passed meds to distract herself.

On Friday, he didn't call to tell her he was at Mercy Hospital, though she knew he was. Plasmaphoresis required several treatments, and today would be his third. She hoped he wouldn't hold a grudge. She had a "date" with him that night—how could she forget? She would stop at her favorite Chinese restaurant on her way over to his house, in the hope of making up for not going to the dialysis unit. She planned to bring him some wonton soup as a peace offering, just in case he was miffed with her.

It seemed a bit silly at first, but the more Mallory thought about it, the more she liked the idea. From home she packed up her daughter's forgotten electric keyboard for JT's musical pleasure. She figured he'd enjoy playing some of his favorite sheet music while he was stuck in bed.

She'd also remembered to bring the wheelchair she'd tucked away in the garage ever since the time Morgan had broken her leg, playing soccer, a few years back. Ever hopeful he'd notice some improvement since the plasmaphoresis, she wanted to be prepared. If she waited for Dr. Berger's order and home health medical equipment delivery, it could take another week to get a wheelchair.

She tucked both items into the trunk of the car and took off for Chinois, the trendy Chinese-European bistro near his house.

She'd been smart and called her order in ahead. Once she arrived, she parked in one of the order pick-up spots and turned off her engine. Just as she was about to open the car door, she recognized two familiar faces approaching—Samantha Prescott and Wayne Berger. His arm rested snugly around her shoulders, and they cuddled in a familiar way. Samantha looked stunning, as always, and Dr. Berger appeared better than usual, as if she'd dressed him. His smile was large and flirtatious and Samantha proffered a dainty giggle over something he'd whispered into her ear.

Feeling as though she were the one betrayed instead of JT, Mallory plopped back against her car seat, blew out her breath and attempted to recover. What the heck should she do now?

Wait it out. Once she'd given them plenty of time to find their dining table, she ventured into the side door of the restaurant to pick up her order.

As she paid, she peered between palm fronds over the divider into the dining room and found them head to head in deep conversation, looking like intimate lovers. Was she reading her own guilt into their friendly little dinner?

Then Dr. Berger dropped a kiss on Samantha's lips.

JT had first become aware of the lack of heaviness in his legs earlier that Friday morning. After he'd completed his last plasmaphoresis treatment that afternoon, he'd noticed it even more. He couldn't describe the subtle change, but welcomed it. Periodically throughout the afternoon he'd tested his mildly receding paralysis, but tried not to become overly optimistic.

While waiting for his favorite nurse at seven p.m., he practiced moving his feet beneath the covers. And they obeyed. He sent a mental message to bend one knee and discovered he could. He wanted to leap out of the bed and do a dance, but knew he'd fall flat on his face if he tried. Instead, he pumped the air with his fist. It was real progress, the first for a while.

Thanks to Mallory and her unyielding desire to get him well, he'd insisted on the treatment that could have helped him recover sooner from the very beginning. Hell, if it hadn't been for her he never would have known they hadn't tried this treatment. He'd been so out of it when he'd first become ill that he hadn't had a clue what they'd tried or hadn't tried for him.

What would he have done if she hadn't been hired to be his nurse? Would he have insisted everyone follow his ridiculous list of rules and let him rot from the inside out in his own house?

Thank God for the adorable scalpel in his side, Mallory.

She burst through the bedroom door with arms loaded, a bag of food and a keyboard. He grinned at her, happier than he'd been in a while. A keyboard? He chuckled at the absurd sight.

"Hi!" She beamed. The balmy summer evening had put an alluring bloom on her face. Her eyes glowed with excitement as her gaze danced around the room.

Simply put, she looked beautiful…and glad to see him. How could he be upset with her for not going to the dialysis unit when he'd called yesterday?

She couldn't possibly know how much her visit meant to him. He didn't want to scare her off, so he'd keep his feelings to himself. "Hey, sunshine," he said, taking a casual tone. "What do you have there?"

"Well, I brought you a blueberry and peach smoothie because of the antioxidants in blueberries, some wonton soup—didn't the speech pathologist check out your swallowing and give you the green light to have thinner liquids this week? Oh, and I have a keyboard."

She put her bags on the dresser near his bed and placed the keyboard on his lap.

"I'll give you time to practice while I go back

to my car. I've got another surprise to bring in. When I get back, I expect you to play me something."

He shook his head at her thoughtfulness and fought off the desire to grab her, kiss her, and push his face into that gorgeous hair. But first he needed to scold her for letting him down yesterday.

She'd bent over, attempting to plug the keyboard into the nearest electrical socket, and all the admonishing thoughts raced out of his head. Nice…pants. She'd worn another pair of snug slacks, which were cropped above the ankle and were eggplant-colored. A dainty silver anklet glistened in the dim light.

She had the kind of shape that excited him. He liked a woman with a little something to grab onto, not the stick-thin women driving the fashion world. Her wispy olive-green top brought out the color of her eyes, making them almost look the color of pine trees tonight. And her hair, what could he say about the beauty of her silky, copper-colored hair? All he wanted to do was run his hands through it. That wasn't exactly true. He also had a powerful urge to run his hands all over her, and kiss every freckle on her face and body—especially the hard-to-find ones.

But she'd plugged the keyboard in and rushed out of the room.

What was this about another surprise? He grinned, looking forward to what she'd do next, and realized he'd been doing a lot more smiling lately.

He forced himself to focus on the silly little instrument on his lap. How could it compare to his baby grand? But the thought was what counted, and he wouldn't let her down. He pressed the "on" button and heard a strange warm-up sound. Poking around on the condensed keyboard, his fingers picked out a tune he thought she might enjoy—the simple yet haunting Erik Satie piece, "First *Gymnopédie*."

When she returned, she left whatever her next surprise was in the hall and leaned respectfully against the doorframe listening, arms folded.

As he continued to play, she approached and sat primly at the foot of his bed, listening raptly to his improvisation.

When he'd finished, she applauded.

"That was lovely," she said with soft eyes.

"Not nearly as lovely as you," he said. "Now that I've earned it, I need a proper greeting."

He saw the hesitation on her face. He knew what she must have been thinking.

"Look, Mallory, when I ask you here on your days off, I need to know you're all mine. I don't want you to battle your brain about what's right and how we are breaking hospital rules. We're not. This is our time, damn it, and I need a kiss before I go insane from not touching you." OK, so he'd stoop to coercion. "And besides, you owe me for not holding my hand through plasmaphoresis. It was all your idea, you know."

She rolled her eyes and shook her head, but took his chastisement to heart. As though she were a gentle healing breeze, she leaned forward and greeted him with a soft, moist kiss on the lips. He inhaled her summery fragrance. The mere touch of her mouth sent a shiver down to his toes. Down to his toes! He'd felt it.

"Now, that's what I'm talking about," he said against her mouth, his arms wrapping around her waist, pulling her closer. "Who needs to eat when I have you to kiss?"

She gave a soft, throaty giggle and kissed him harder, then, just when he'd gotten carried away with wild thoughts of seducing her on his hospital bed, she pulled back. A serious-as-hell stare doused his fantasy.

"Too bad I'm famished. We'll have to pick this up again after I've eaten," she said.

"You're a tease. That's what you are."

The aroma of Chinese food had filled his nostrils when she'd entered. He couldn't deny it had awakened his appetite, but Mallory was something he wanted much more. He'd have to wait for the right time and place, and hope his body could catch up with his desires. In the meantime, there was always food. Delicious. Glorious. Food.

"So what's the big surprise?" he asked later, between sips of salty noodles and pork.

Her eyes widened. She daintily bit into a spring roll, chewed and swallowed. "It's a wheelchair. I thought we'd go for an evening spin to your back yard. There's supposed to be meteor showers over the next few nights. Maybe we can catch some."

"That's a great idea." He definitely had a few shooting-star ideas of his own for later, in the dark…with her…just to show his gratitude.

His regular weekday nurse, Gloria, had left for her dinner-break when Mallory had arrived, on JT's instructions. But once Mallory had finished eating, she went searching for Gloria.

"I think, between you and me, we should be able to transfer J—uh, Dr. Prescott, to the wheelchair. What do you think?"

"I'm game."

Anxious to try out his newfound strength, JT nodded with agreement.

Mallory had him sit up straight, then swiveled his legs to the edge of the bed before dropping his feet to the floor.

"Now, just sit there a minute and dangle while you adjust to standing up."

"We'll be holding you up, so don't worry about not being strong enough," Gloria chimed in.

Mallory moved the wheelchair parallel to the

bed, and stood directly in front of JT. "You be on standby, Gloria. I'm going to pull him up and pivot him around to back into the chair. If his feet buckle, I'll need you to help me lift him in.

"Are your legs still feeling like wet noodles?" Mallory glanced into his face before grabbing him in an around-the-waist bear hug.

"Not really."

"Great!" She pulled back and searched his eyes for the meaning of what he'd just said.

He gave her an I'm-not-telling smile.

"Put your arms around my shoulders," she said.

"Gladly, but don't forget Gloria is watching," he said with a deadpan face.

"Get over yourself, big guy. Now, stand on the count of three. One, two, three!"

Mallory pulled him up to a standing position and for the first time he was able to will his legs to stay straight. The soles of his feet felt the hard cold floor when she swiveled him. Hallelujah! Gloria stayed nearby to support him from the side. His knees didn't buckle. Before he could finish thinking *three*, Mallory had him settled in the wheelchair.

A startled look widened her eyes. "That went really smoothly."

He grinned at her. "I think the plasmaphoresis is doing its job. I can feel my feet again."

"Oh, my God!" She took his face in her hands and gave him the sweetest, most triumphant smile he'd ever seen. "It worked?" Her comforting fingers sent electricity across his neck and shoulders. The moisture in her eyes sent another message altogether.

He nodded, marveling at the inner beauty he'd come to adore about Mallory. Was the swell of euphoria from the receding paralysis or from the look of love in her eyes?

He swallowed the emotion. When had he last felt this way about anyone? He needed time to digest the rush of feelings snapping to life in his head and heart. He'd have to sort them out later.

Before him, Mallory did the bugaloo celebration dance he'd wanted to do himself earlier. He liked her version much better.

After she'd calmed down she hung his IV on a portable pole and connected to the wheelchair, placed a light blanket across his lap and rolled him outside to his patio. How long had it been since he'd seen his own house?

Jake had kept the yard in perfect order, with the tall bushes well trimmed and the flowers flourishing. One particular hibiscus bush was covered in bright single-layer red blooms, each open like a five-petal smile.

The night sky was a shadowed blue, yet several stars already shone brightly. The yard accent lights would have to be turned off if they were to star-gaze.

Gloria had followed them both outside.

"Gloria? As Mallory is here, I'm going to let you leave early tonight—full pay, of course."

"Why, thank you, Dr. Prescott."

She left almost before he could say goodnight. "Oh, and on your way out, can you turn off the accent lights?"

Once the coast was clear and the yard was dark, he reached for Mallory's hand.

"It's beautiful out tonight, isn't it?" she said.

"Fantastic. And only one thing will make it perfect."

Playing along, she looked coyly at him. "Why,

Dr. Prescott, what could that possibly be? Do you want the keyboard so you can serenade me?"

He tugged her closer. "What I really want is for you to sit on my lap."

After a surprised glance she obliged him. She felt all female across his thighs, and when she circled her arms around his neck, he thought he'd been reborn.

High on life and Mallory, he gazed into her fathomless eyes, smiled richly, and kissed her.

They kissed like teenagers in the back seat of a car, all hot and eager to thrill each other, easily aroused. He wished there were no blanket barriers between them. She grasped his head, fingers diving into his hair, and held him close as her tongue explored his lips. It made him growl and kiss her back—deeper. The sweet taste of almond cookies lingered in her mouth. Her warm breath sent a direct signal across his flesh, all the way down to his groin.

When had a woman last done that to him? He couldn't remember any of their faces, except for Mallory's. Right here. Right now.

His hand ran from her waist up her side, and was about to sample the soft flesh of her breast when he heard the familiar shuffling gait of Jake coming around the corner of the house.

Would he ever have his privacy back? He gave one quick squeeze and flick of his thumb then backed off. A cheap thrill, he'd admit, but enticing all the same.

Mallory quickly rose to a standing position, and for the first time that night he was glad he had a blanket across his lap.

"Hiya, boss. Beautiful night. I came to see why the back-yard lights were turned off."

Mallory subtly smoothed her clothes and hair, and gave the guiltiest smile he'd ever seen for Jake. It almost made JT chuckle.

"Pull up a chair and join us. We were just star-gazing," JT said.

"Sure thing, but where is Mallory sitting?"

A mischievous glance from his dream date made him sputter a laugh. "How about on my lap?"

"Oh, you," Mallory said, with a friendly cuff to his shoulder, as though the idea was preposterous.

"Right," Jake said, all business. "Let me get a chair for her, too."

Not having a clue how he'd dampened their passion, Jake sat in staid silence, staring at the cobalt sky. Occasionally, he'd clear his throat.

JT decided he'd had enough, and asked to be wheeled inside. Fortunately Jake didn't follow them back into the house. It was twenty to nine and there were a few minutes remaining until his night nurse, Carlos, arrived. He hoped to have a chance to kiss Mallory again tonight, but this time the way he really wanted to.

Shaken by the passion she'd felt between them in his back yard, Mallory was grateful for Jake having barged in earlier. Where would their kisses have led? And when JT had caressed her breast, she'd almost called out with the surge of desire.

It had to stop.

"Let's get you back to bed, shall we?" Mallory said, all business. Oh, damn. That hadn't come out like she'd meant it.

"I like that idea, but only if you'll join me."

She cast him a shocked stare.

Her mind had wandered back to the Samantha and Wayne sighting from earlier that evening, and she wondered how best to broach the subject, or whether to let it be.

JT's brow knitted with a perplexed look. "What happened to little miss wildcat from outside? I liked her better."

She gave him the sincerest expression she could conjure up. "I'm just not sure what to do about us. Are we just playing around? Or are you really interested in me?"

He took her hand in his and stared into her eyes. "I trust you more than anyone I know— besides myself, of course. Please, believe me when I say I'm definitely interested in you. Hell, I think about you all the time. This isn't warped gratitude for everything you've done for me. Not that I'm not grateful. It's just so much more than that. Please, get that through your beautiful head. Now, put me to bed. And, if you'd like, you can join me."

She sighed over her outburst of nerves. The sincerity in his eyes took her breath away. He'd pretty much laid it on the line, and now it was up to her how she wanted to reciprocate.

"At least tuck me in," he whispered in a husky voice.

Mallory fought to ignore the chills running rampant on her skin. She locked the wheelchair in place, used her thighs and a straight back to lower herself to his level, and reached behind his waist. His arms naturally wrapped around her shoulders sending, a warm wave over her back.

"On the count of three we'll stand. Pivot to the right, I mean your left, then you can sit on the edge of the bed while I get the wheelchair out of the way. Then I'll help lift your legs. OK. One…two…three!"

He managed to make it to standing with little effort and her help. They did a dance of three short steps until the backs of his knees were pushed up flush to the bed. He was supposed to sit, but momentum from the sitting-to-standing movement must have made him lose his balance. He fell backwards onto the bed and, having never released her, she tumbled on top of him.

Now sprawled across his body, on his bed, still

firmly in his embrace, she pushed up onto her hands to figure out what had happened. He smiled devilishly up at her, his blue eyes blazing with desire. He pulled her back down flush to his body and she became urgently aware that their hips were together in a most provocative place.

Shock coursed through her. She tried with all her resistance not to move, but she felt him throb to life beneath her. His mouth found hers in a hot, wet kiss, and in a mind-numbing response she straddled him.

They'd picked right up where they'd left off outside. Wild kisses and nibbles on the neck, each with a sweet wake-up message sent directly to her core. His hands found her breasts again— this time they explored her shape and feel. Her flesh tightened and pebbled beneath his fingers, and she grew wet between her legs. And, oh, that connection at the hip—the firm bulge was too much to resist.

She moved over him in sweet, deep undulations, their lips never losing contact. His hands made their way up the back of her blouse and managed to unclasp her bra. He released her, and she marveled at the feel of his warm hands on her flesh. She threw her head back and arched into his grip, savoring the feel. A tiny moan escaped her lips.

One of his hands pressed her tightly down on top of him. She gasped her pleasure. He pulled her close and ran a tingling course across her neck, and found a spot to kiss that sent fireworks throughout her belly. He kissed harder and she thought she might cry out. She pressed deeper onto him with a slow shimmy, while she lifted his hospital gown and ran her fingers over the crinkly curls of his chest. God, he felt good.

Stomach to stomach, her hand slipped down his ribs to his waist and finally to embrace his length, and savor the tight and smooth skin, hard and ready.

Driven with desire, she said, "I want you," though she was shocked to hear herself say it.

In a flash his hands were at her zipper, pulling her slacks down over her hips. He'd gotten them just low enough to where the tip of him found her wet flesh. She pressed against him, overcome with excitement, unable to wait another second to feel him inside her.

She rose to her knees to help remove the rest of her slacks when a rap on the front door brought her to her senses.

Oh, my God. What was she doing? The night nurse was here!

On Saturday morning Mallory blushed at the thought of seeing JT again. He'd given her the sexiest smile she'd ever seen when she'd left the night before. And after all they'd done, and had almost done, how could she face him? Maybe she should give up the job. But she needed the money. It was just all too confusing.

She brushed her hair with hard strokes and pulled it so firmly back into a ponytail that her eyes slanted upward. She wrapped the hair around and around into a tight little bun. Next she put on her most unbecoming nursing uniform and thick white support hose, even though it was summer. She topped things off with a drab beige sweater. Nothing, absolutely nothing would be exposed.

Off to work she'd go, business before pleasure, completely doubtful of her resolve.

When she arrived, JT had done just the opposite. He'd had the night nurse help him clean up; he'd shaved but left a sexy-as-hell Zen patch beneath his lower lip. He'd put on a summery Hawaiian shirt instead of the hospital gown. There was fire in his deep blue eyes when she walked in. She couldn't survive the day under that heat.

"Good morning, Carlos. Dr. Prescott." She nodded without making eye contact. "I'm back on duty," she said with a prudish smile. "On duty, got that?"

She flitted around the room, opening curtains, straightening books on tabletops, odds and ends on bookcases, adjusting pictures on walls.

Not betraying an ounce of disappointment, JT shook hands with Carlos, bade him goodday and waited for Mallory to face him.

"OK. I get it. You can relax now." He sat taller in bed and crossed his arms. "Put me in the chair. I want to visit my real piano."

"Let me take your vital signs first."

Relieved to have a purpose, and hoping she wouldn't crack under JT's alluring spell, Mallory brought him upright and performed the three-step pivot dance until he'd settled into the wheel-chair. Though the feel of his body so close to hers was torture, today the move had gone even more easily. Was it possible to recover so quickly from GBS after such a long plateau? Soon he wouldn't need her or anyone to care for him.

"I'll change the linen and get your meds ready while you're in the living room."

"Fine."

Though wanting to explain her confusion to him, she chewed her lower lip and rolled him out the door in silence. He sat straight and stared ahead.

She pushed the piano bench aside and rolled him up to the keys, then dutifully lifted the lid and set up the support.

"Can I get you anything before I go?"

One hand fingered a couple of keys. He stared in reserved concentration.

Taking his reticence as a no, she turned to leave.

"The woman I held in my arms last night," he said softly as she walked away.

Her crêpe sole tangled on the throw rug but she caught herself and faced him.

A nervous hand ran over her hair. "Look, JT, I'm totally confused about how to behave around you. I'm here to work today. We can't maintain the sort of relationship we had last night when I'm on duty. It's not acceptable to me."

"I understand. Just admit that you feel something for me. I want to hear it." He stared so deeply into her eyes she thought she might lose her balance.

"I can't go to sleep at night without seeing your face. I think about you all week at work. You jump into my mind at the oddest times. I've lost any hope of hiding it, or resisting you. What more do you need to know?"

"That you take me seriously when I tell you I want you in my life."

This was too much to face on a Saturday morning. She had eleven hours more to face JT. He'd just dropped a bombshell, which under other circumstances would have had her dancing in the street. But she was at work, and it was of utmost importance to maintain a professional attitude. And she was so confused. Could she trust that he wouldn't lose interest in her once she'd given in and let herself feel everything brewing in her heart for him?

"I do, JT. It's just now isn't the time to talk about it."

With that, she turned and left the room.

Mallory worked furiously to distract herself. She prepared his morning medicine and changed the bedlinen. She couldn't help stopping from time to time to sway with the beauty of the sonata coming from the living room. She fantasized about a lifetime of hearing him play the piano—a lifetime with him. Dared she dream such a thing?

When she came to his pillow, she pulled off the case and a photo fell out—the one of her with her blouse off her shoulder, trying to look sexy but falling far short. The gesture of him keeping her photograph under his pillow cracked her hard resolve and she smiled for the first time that morning. She did mean something to him, though she had yet to sort it all out. She placed the photo on the bedside table and finished her job. She wanted JT back in bed before Dr. Berger arrived for his daily visit. She'd tell him all about her fears and worries then.

She'd just finished fluffing the pillow and smoothing the bedspread when she heard a crash from the other room. She ran out the door and into the living room to find JT sitting on the floor, his hand covering his eye. She rushed to his side.

"Are you all right?"

"Dammit!" he said. "I shouldn't have tried to stand on my own, but I wanted to get some other music."

"Let me have a look." She eased his hand away and saw blood oozing from his brow. She knew that heads and brows bled more easily than other parts of the body, but this looked bad. He must have caught it on the corner of the table on his way down to the floor.

"Stay right there, and press on it," she said. "I'm going to get something to clean it with. You may need a stitch or two."

Mallory lunged for the supplies while drops of

blood stained his shirt. She flew back into the hallway just as Dr. Berger arrived.

"What's going on?" he asked.

"Dr. Prescott has fallen. I'm going to clean him up."

He followed hot on her heels. "What the hell is he doing out here? Was he left alone?"

JT spoke up. "I made the decision to stand on my own, and I fell. That's all there is to it."

Dr. Berger squinted and tossed Mallory an incredulous look. "You left him alone?"

"Look, I'm not an invalid without a brain. She had nothing to do with my stupidity."

Ignoring the doctor to tend to her patient, Mallory dropped to her knees and pressed gauze to his brow. "Wipe your hands on this." She gave him a damp washcloth. "Does it hurt?"

"I'm fine."

"He wanted to play the piano, so I went back to change his bedlinen. I'm so sorry this happened."

"Get the wheelchair," Dr. Berger commanded, placing his medical bag on the couch. "And where did he get a wheelchair? I haven't ordered one. Once again, I'm astounded by your poor judgement, Nurse Glenn. You consistently overstep your bounds."

"Knock it off, Wayne. I already told you this was my decision. Now, either shut up or get out."

Strained silence followed as they all worked to put JT back into his chair. Once everything was in order, Mallory rolled him into his bedroom.

In the bright sunlight, after washing his hands, Dr. Berger examined JT's eye. "I think a stitch and a couple of butterfly bandages should do it. Nurse Glenn, clean this area with Betadine." He fished through his bag and found what he needed while she did as she was told. When he'd finished his job, he said, "Let's get him back to bed."

Mallory rolled the wheelchair to the bedside and locked the brakes. She noticed the picture of herself on the table and thought quickly about slipping it into her pocket as soon as JT was back in bed. "OK, just the way we've practiced before, Dr. Prescott. On the count of three."

JT stood and Wayne Berger watched without offering a hand. Mallory danced him around and sat him on the edge of the bed. Her mind couldn't help remembering what had happened the last time they'd attempted this maneuver together. A hot flush snaked up her neck. JT worked the muscle in his jaw, but kept silent. Was he recalling their near sex, too?

Mallory stepped back to remove the wheelchair and pick up the picture, but it was too late. She'd caught Dr. Berger's gaze firmly on the photo. He lifted his eyes with a slow accusatory glare. Oh, how she wanted to bust him and his little fling, too. But she was the underdog here, and until she figured out how JT felt about his ex-wife, she'd keep her mouth shut.

"Is there something going on here?" Dr. Berger asked.

JT lifted a brow and glanced at the photo in Mallory's hand halfway from table to pocket.

"I got bored. I took some pictures. That's all."

"Since when does your nurse dress like that to come to work?"

"She came on her day off, at my invitation. Whatever we do on our own time is none of your business."

Dr. Berger gave Mallory a cold glance, judgement glinting in his eyes. "This is highly unethical, Ms. Glenn. If you insist on seducing your patients, you have no place in home health, or the hospital for that matter."

"Back off, Wayne. Mallory is an excellent nurse and a boon to Mercy Hospital. We need more nurses like her."

The rest of the examination took place in cool silence and thick tension. Mallory left the room to get a drink of water and regroup. She'd have to be very careful with her personal time and involvement in JT's life from now on if she wanted to keep her job. And after today, because she needed the money, she promised to keep things strictly businesslike. But how was she supposed to do that when she had the rest of the day and several hours' worth of physical therapy exercises to take him through?

Being a nurse for fifteen years, she'd had to learn to shut down the attraction or growing friendships with patients. She knew how to do it, and she'd use every evasive skill in her repertoire to make it through the day.

"He has a lot of nerve, chastising you when

he's the biggest flirt I've ever seen at work. He used to think the nursing staff was his own personal dating pool," JT said later that day while she assisted with his leg exercises.

"I don't think he's interested in nurses any more." It slipped out before she could catch herself.

"You mean the fact that he has a thing for my ex-wife? Is that the hospital gossip?"

"No. I've never heard anything about it at work."

"What are you getting at, Mallory? Do you know something I don't?"

"No." She tried to keep busy, fussing with things near his bed to distract her gaze, but his large hand wrapped around hers and put a quick end to it.

"I know Samantha sees other men, if that's what you're getting at. I also know she wants full custody of Corey."

OK, why not? He had his suspicions anyway. "Actually, last night when I picked up the food, I saw them together at Chinois. They looked… involved."

"Involved as in conversation?"

"Involved as in…kissing."

An expression of complete understanding burned on his cheeks. "That leech wants my job *and* my ex-wife."

On Sunday morning Samantha delivered Corey for the all-day visit, as she'd promised. She kissed him goodbye and reminded him she'd be back in four hours.

"Any plans for your free time, Sammy?" JT asked.

She looked uneasy, and maybe a bit surprised. "I'll probably go shopping."

"Ah. Don't forget the credit card. Oh, have you changed it to your own name yet?"

She shot daggers from narrow angry eyes, turned on her heel and left without a word.

Oblivious, or at least pretending to be unaware of the tension between his parents, Corey came bounding up to his father, who was sitting in the wheelchair near the window.

"Hey, bud," JT said, opening his arms.

"Dad, I've told you not to call me that."

"Oh, right. Hey, *dude,* check this out." He lifted a knee and kicked out his foot.

"Wow! You're getting better."

They hugged.

"You bet I am. Pretty soon you'll be able to spend the whole weekend with me, just like before."

"Cool. What happened to your eye?"

Early shades of blue-green and purple painted his brow beneath the tiny bandages. "A brow piercing gone wrong."

"Ah, come on, Dad. You'd never get your eyebrow pierced."

"OK. I was stupid and tried to stand by myself. I guess I'm not quite ready to do that yet."

"It's a good thing your nurse was around."

"Hi, Corey," Mallory said. "Remember me?" She'd noticed the boy had combed his hair down instead of in the trendy *faux* Mohawk hairdo from last weekend.

"Yeah, you're the think-fast nurse."

She giggled and handed him another gizmo. "Yep. And today I'll need your help with this. Your dad has to squeeze it twelve times in each hand four different times. I need you to make sure he doesn't cheat or quit."

"I'm on it," he said, snatching it up. "This

looks like a pair of pliers." He tried pressing it shut. "Wow. This is really stiff."

Later, when she'd put JT back on the bed, she showed Corey how to work his father's right leg while she exercised the left one. Corey never complained. In fact, he worked earnestly to help his dad. Father and son carried on a relaxed banter throughout, and in the strangest way she felt a part of their little family.

"Am I helping you get well, Dad?"

"You bet you are."

"And Nurse Think Fast is too."

"Right again."

Against her better judgement, but wanting Corey to see more progress with his father's recovery, Mallory summoned Jake to assist with getting JT into the wheelchair again. Dr. Berger be damned.

"Listen, boss, if you don't mind, I'd like to take the afternoon off."

"Sure. You should do that more often, Jake. You have a hot date?"

The old man laughed. "A friend got me some tickets to the Dodgers baseball game."

"Enjoy."

After lunch, Mallory could tell that Corey was getting a little restless so she suggested they all go out back and take in some sunshine. Corey ran to his own bedroom in the house and found two baseball mitts and a large soft ball. JT brought his camera.

"Hey, Dad, will you play catch?"

"Sure thing, dude. But first, want me to show you how to take really good pictures?"

"Yeah!"

An hour later JT gave Mallory a beseeching look. "You know what I'd really like about now?"

Oh, God, please, don't say "a kiss" in front of your son.

"An ice-cream cone."

"Me, too. Me, too," Corey chimed in.

"But we don't have any cones here, I don't think," she said.

"There's an ice-cream store three blocks away. If I pay, will you drive?"

"I can't leave you alone. I'm on duty!"

"Please, Nurse, please, bring us ice creams."

She glared at JT for planting the thought in his son's head. He perceived her message.

"Listen, Mallory, I promise not to move or try to get up. One fall for the week is enough. Corey will hold me to it. Right, Corey?"

"Yeah. I promise to look after my dad."

How could she resist the huge blue eyes of Corey, the image of his father when he looked at her like that?

Assessing the situation, father and son playing catch in the back yard—one of them a mature adult who was no longer completely helpless, the other a good, though occasionally rambunctious kid—she decided it would be OK to make a quick ice-cream run.

"Oh, OK. But I'm leaving your cellphone with you. I'll only be gone fifteen minutes. Not a second longer, I promise. Now what flavors do you want?"

The ice-cream store was packed, and it took closer to thirty minutes to buy the treats and drive back to the Prescott house. Mallory's heart sank when she arrived and recognized Dr. Berger's car, and in front of it Samantha's Jaguar.

CHAPTER SIX

MALLORY parked the car, gathered the cardboard transport box with the three cones in small cups, and took a deep breath. She'd need all the nerve she could call up. How could she explain to Dr. Berger and Samantha Prescott that she hadn't been negligent, neither had she abandoned her job, when she'd left the premises while on duty?

She couldn't.

Her stomach cramped, and she closed her eyes. "I've totally blown it." With her arms covered in anxious tingles, she bit her lower lip to keep it from quivering. She shook her head, hoping to generate an idea.

Having left JT and Corey out back, she got out of the car and retraced her steps to the backyard down the red-brick walk at the side of the house.

If she ever got sent before a firing squad, she suspected it would feel something like this.

She heard quarreling long before she reached the gate.

"What if you'd had an emergency?" said Dr. Berger in a grating voice. "What would that trauma do to your son?"

Oh, no. Please, don't drag Corey into this fight. Don't force him to take sides or be in the middle of your manipulation. Had Dr. Berger any knowledge of child psychology? He was making Corey feel guilty about loving his father. *Please, don't make him take sides.*

She leaned against the garage wall to gather her wits and listened to the voices raised in anger.

"What if he'd fallen and hurt himself?" came Samantha's shrill response.

"I have a cellphone, Samantha. I'm not an idiot."

"I…I just wanted an ice-cream cone," Corey said, sounding forlorn.

"This just shows that I can't trust Corey with you ever again," Samantha said, her voice rising. "I've said it before, but now I'm adamant. I want total custody."

"Now is not the time to have this conversation." JT's booming response forced everyone into silence.

With the lull, Mallory took a deep breath, opened the creaking cedar gate and drew everyone's attention her way. Dr. Berger and Samantha glared at her. Corey looked torn about his ice cream, and stopped himself from running up to her after a few steps.

The knot in her stomach grew to the size of a soccer ball.

JT sat straight and proud in the wheelchair, sunlight shining in his raven hair. He clenched his jaw and didn't so much as glance her way.

Was JT so ready to dismiss her? What about everything he'd said? Pain cut like a searing dagger through her chest. So her fears had been justified. He wanted a playmate, someone to distract him while he healed, but when things got sticky he would cut her free.

She could hardly breathe, but she was damned if she'd give Samantha, Dr. Berger and, most especially, JT the satisfaction of seeing her come apart in front of them.

"I suppose there is no explaining why I left the premises."

"As a matter of fact, no," Dr. Berger said with a cutting tone. "Consider yourself fired and pack up."

"Knock it off, Wayne. She works for me, and I'll make that decision." JT used his strong forearms to spin the wheelchair in Wayne's direction.

"I beg to differ, JT. She works for Mercy Hospital and I'm your attending physician. I deem her guilty of dereliction of duty." Dr. Berger leaned forward, invading JT's space. "I believe you authored that regulation in hospital protocol yourself." He turned his head and stared Mallory down as though he was a deer hunter taking aim. "You're not to work with Dr. Prescott again. And I'm not sure you'll have a job at Mercy Hospital either, when this is all over."

She caught herself from dropping the ice cream. "Corey? Would you like your cone?" For the boy's sake, she willed herself to stay calm and composed, though her hands were flapping enough to turn the ice cream into milkshakes.

Corey edged her way, until Samantha stopped him cold with an admonishing glare.

"Dr. Prescott?" Mallory knew ice cream was the last thing on his mind at this moment, but she had to look at him to see where he stood. He didn't respond. Not with her apparently. "Right, I'll get my things."

Crushed by his passive response, she fought the stinging behind her eyelids. She was damned if she'd let him see how much he'd hurt her. Why had she let herself believe all his flattery—and that was all that it had been—when he'd used her for his own pleasure? How could she have been so stupid? And, most importantly, where was JT now when she needed someone in her corner? He didn't even have the decency to look at her.

Disheartened and defeated, Mallory made an about-face, dumped the ice cream into the trashcan at the side of the house, and used the garage entrance to go inside to retrieve her nurse's bag and what was left of her pride.

She'd blown her job, big time, and there was no wriggling out of this one. But, far worse, she'd let herself down by trusting the wrong man. The best thing she could do right now was pack up and leave.

And tomorrow she hoped her nursing position at Mercy Hospital wouldn't be the next job she got fired from.

"I need to use the bathroom. Take me inside," JT said, staring down Wayne. He'd wait until Corey was well out of earshot before he unloaded his anger on Berger.

"I'm going to take Corey home now. I'll get you some ice cream, sweetie. Don't worry," Samantha said, sweeter than sugar.

"Corey? Come here, son."

The boy moved with hesitation, as though afraid to make anyone angry with him. Damn. JT didn't want to add to his grief, but he wanted to make sure the boy knew he wasn't in trouble and wasn't to blame.

When Corey reached him, he opened his arms to give him a hug. "None of this is your fault. Don't think for one second that it is."

Corey's narrow shoulders stiffened and he nodded his head. "I just wanted ice cream."

Corey fought back tears, and JT's heart gripped so hard he thought it might explode from the pressure. "I did, too, and there was nothing wrong with that." He rubbed his son's back. "You know how sometimes we talk about making good choices in life? Well, I guess I didn't do such a good job today. I'm sorry."

"That's OK, Dad. I still love you."

"Kiss your father goodbye. We're leaving." Samantha commanded.

Kiss my ass, Sammy. That's what he wanted to say, but this time he made the right choice and kept his mouth shut. That was after he said, "I love you too, Corey."

So he'd lost his woman and son for a stinking ice-cream cone. Who'd ever have guessed?

"Wayne, roll me inside," he said after they'd left. "I need to go to the bathroom."

Wayne looked irritated, like it just dawned on him that he was "it" until home health provided another caregiver. He reluctantly rolled JT inside, and handed him the container to urinate in.

Once Berger had washed his hands, he got on

his cellphone and made contact with the home health representative. After he'd arranged for a temporary replacement for Mallory, he rolled JT back toward his bed, then stood there with his hands in his pockets, as if JT could jump from wheelchair to bed without any assistance.

"Help me out here." JT was determined to keep his cool, though he'd chewed the inside of his mouth until he'd drawn blood.

Looking awkward, Wayne assessed the situation with shifty eyes. "What do you want me to do?"

"Pull me up and pivot me around so I can sit on the bed."

They performed a clumsy dance but managed to land JT on his bed. Interesting. He caught a potent whiff of Samantha's favorite overpriced perfume on Wayne's golf shirt. Maybe they'd spent the afternoon together while Corey had been here? But why had they come to pick him up early? If they'd only arrived twenty minutes later, this fiasco could have been avoided.

"Now lift my legs for me."

Once JT was on his bed he asked for a glass of water to get Wayne out of the room so he could think straight. How was he supposed to save Mallory's neck when he'd written the hospital protocol? The coppery taste of blood reminded him to quit chewing the inside of his mouth. And how the hell was he going to explain to her why he'd left her for the wolves? Somehow he had to get back in control of his life.

When Wayne returned with the drink, he grimaced and scratched his neck as he handed it over, looking like he had something he wanted to add to their prior conversation.

"You may think fraternizing with your nurse is OK, but Mercy Hospital will have no part of it." He set the glass on the bedside table.

JT grabbed Wayne by the collar and yanked him down to his eye level, surprised by his own burst of strength. "What about *you* fraternizing with my wife, Wayne? Is that acceptable? Would Mercy Hospital be interested in hearing about that?"

JT let go after a long, heated staring contest. Wayne cautiously stood up and straightened his shirt. "She's your ex-wife, if you recall," he growled.

"She wasn't when you started seeing her. We both know that. And Hospital Medical Director is *not* my ex-job." He jabbed the air with his finger. "Don't forget it."

Wayne backed away from the bed. Sure, JT had been thinking about giving up the job for a full-time medical practice again, but over his dead body would he hand the medical director-ship over to Wayne.

"And, furthermore, I'm firing you. From now on Joel Hersh will be my personal physician."

"I'm sure hospital administration will be most interested in seeing this little photograph I found." Wayne dug into his pants pocket. "I believe you took it?" He flashed the photo of Mallory with her blouse off her shoulder. "Or maybe this one, too." He pulled out a blurred black and white photo of the two of them kissing on his bed, when she'd come to visit him last Tuesday night.

JT froze. The second picture had obviously been taken from the surveillance video camera. How much more had they seen?

He thought Jake had turned the system off at his order when he'd been able to talk again. And who had access to his personal camera besides Jake?

Whose side was Jake on?

Crushed by the knowledge he couldn't trust anyone, and that the only person he dared trust had just gotten fired because he'd been too much of a coward to stick up for her, JT shut down his mind in exchange for emotional paralysis.

"We can strike a deal. Right now," Wayne said cautiously. "It has come to my attention that Mallory used a part-time chart-room employee to read your inpatient medical records. That violation of the hospital privacy act alone will ensure she gets fired."

"I gave her permission," JT lied.

"Rubbish! I know you've got the hots for her, and that she has a daughter away at college. I'll make sure the nurse keeps her job at Mercy, and you can screw her all you want, as far as I'm concerned, if you'll turn the medical directorship over to me, and Corey over to Samantha."

"Go to hell, Berger. I don't do blackmail."

* * *

Late that night, Mallory tossed and turned in bed. Her lack of professionalism had cost her the extra job, and she was afraid she'd lose her full-time hospital job, too. She'd rushed into a relationship with a patient, a big no-no, and needed to backpedal for a while.

JT had let her down so hard that her wounds would need months to heal. Why couldn't she have figured it out before she'd gotten hurt?

What was it about JT that had made her cross the line? It wasn't his chiseled features—she'd come to him when he'd looked his worse. It wasn't money or power—he'd been at his weakest. It wasn't charm—he'd been vile toward her at first.

Perhaps it was the look of a fighter she'd identified with. She knew how to never give up, and though he appeared to have completely withdrawn and given in to his disease, she'd seen the glimmer of a warrior in his cold, hard stare when he'd lain helpless in his hospital bed. At first he'd mistakenly directed the fiery look toward her, but as time had gone on those cobalt blue eyes had softened and invited her into his stronghold. That's when she'd slipped under his spell. The day he'd accepted her.

Thoughts of JT and the time and intimacy they'd shared, tears, hurt, and frustration kept her from sleeping.

Morgan had moved into the dorm at college two weeks earlier, and the house felt painfully empty. She had no one to talk to, and the one person she craved to discuss this mess with was the last person she could ever contact again, if she wanted to keep her job. But apparently JT wasn't prepared to risk anything for a relationship with her.

Tears flowed down her cheeks, but nothing could wash away the pain. How foolish of her to ever think she could have what she'd always wanted—a loving relationship with a man— without paying a price.

Her dreary life of all work and no play had little appeal. But back to her sad reality she'd go, grateful to have a job—at least, if Mercy Hospital agreed to keep her on staff.

Starting tomorrow, JT couldn't exist in her world. She owed it to her daughter who had tuition to pay, and she owed it to herself. The pain of never seeing him again, never taking care of him or laughing with him, was much less than if she'd allowed herself to succumb to him and he'd broken her heart on top of letting her down.

Too bad she'd already fallen in love.

The stern look of the nursing supervisor scared the life out of Mallory on Monday morning. She had never felt more vulnerable, yet face her she did, forcing a smile and praying for mercy.

Short silver hair framed round cheeks and gray eyes that usually smiled when they saw Mallory, but not today. Today her supervisor's eyes flashed.

"You'll be on probation for three months. If any extracurricular activity with any of your patients comes to my attention, you'll be fired. No questions asked.

"It's a good thing you have had excellent reviews from every department you've ever worked in, your co-workers sing your praises, and we are in the midst of a nursing shortage. Your patient care expertise has literally saved your tail this time. Now, go back to work, and keep your nose clean."

Mallory could breathe again. She wouldn't be pounding the pavement, searching for a job, with a sordid reputation following her everywhere she went. She wouldn't have to pull Morgan from her dream university and have her enroll in the local community college. The only price she'd have to pay was never seeing JT again.

Somehow she felt as though she was getting a lousy deal.

For the following month, JT worked at his laptop, insisting on doing part of his medical director's duties from home. Each day he grew stronger and, other than physical therapy four hours a day, all other medical treatment had stopped. He was eating on his own, and even using a walker to get around. It only made sense to pick up some of his duties while he continued to recover. Otherwise he'd spend all of his time thinking about Mallory and driving himself crazy, missing her.

The hardest part of all was staying out of

contact with her. But it was for her own good. He'd done nothing but mess up her life, and he owed her a little peace of mind. Yeah, it was much better just to let things lie for now.

He hadn't seen Corey in two weeks and he looked forward to the upcoming supervised weekend visit. It would be the second visit since the big blow-up. Samantha dangled the boy over his head like a carrot, but little did she know he'd consulted his attorney and the battle for custody was anything but over.

Samantha had started out as ideal wife material. She'd come from a privileged family, just like him. She'd graduated from the perfect college, just like him. She'd dabbled in charity fundraising, which sounded good for a doctor's wife. And she looked great—the perfect trophy wife, as his father once told him. She had even been good in the bedroom, but they'd never connected the way he and Mallory had. Nowhere close. And he and Mallory had never even made love! No, he'd never called Samantha his soulmate, but Mallory?

Funny, he'd never believed in the idea of a

soul-mate, but lately he'd been rethinking the topic.

Back when he'd married Samantha it had all been about getting ahead, prestige, and power—a soul-mate had been the last thing he'd looked for.

He'd made her sign a prenuptial agreement to protect his family's wealth, and she'd never forgiven him. And once she'd given birth to Corey, things had never been the same. All she'd wanted had been a bigger and bigger paycheck. How shallow he'd been to marry a woman who claimed charitable fundraising as a career. Thank God he'd finally seen through his errors, and when she'd set her sights on Wayne Berger, he'd filed for divorce.

Samantha had gotten half of everything he'd accrued as a doctor during the course of their marriage in their divorce settlement. Once Corey turned eighteen, she'd be cut back to a mere couple of grand a month. Never having held an actual paid job in her life, no wonder she was chasing Wayne Berger. Her gravy train would run out in eight years.

With several suspicions about Wayne and

Samantha spying and conspiring to set him up, he had now developed a few plans of his own, and his attorney was very optimistic about his and Corey's future under the same roof.

Only one major problem stood in the way. He couldn't see Mallory again. Not if he wanted his son.

He hadn't seen Mallory in over a month, and he ached to touch her again, to run his hands across her body. He missed her cheerful, chirpy manner and aggravatingly cute ways every single day. And most of all he missed her beautiful smile. But he had no choice, his attorney had warned him.

The only thing he wanted more than to walk again was to see Mallory.

At least he could rest assured knowing he'd done the most he could on her behalf. After a private phone call to the hospital administrator and the nursing director last month, both of whom owed him a favor or two, Mercy Hospital had agreed to keep her on staff.

And he'd paid Morgan's first-year tuition in full. It didn't help missing Mallory one bit, but at least he'd given her something. She deserved much, much more.

He pulled the pictures of Mallory out of his drawer, promising himself it would be the last time he dwelt on memories of their first date almost six weeks ago. What he'd give to run his fingers through her silky soft hair and kiss her pert mouth again. If only…

"You wanted me, boss?" Jake appeared at his study door in his familiar gray uniform.

"Yeah." JT tucked the pictures away, and switched back to reality. "I wanted to ask you a few questions."

The stocky, stalwart fix-it man placed a gnarled hand on his hip. "Sure, shoot."

"Do you still have the letter I gave you about shutting down the ventilator if my condition worsened?"

"Yes. It's in my safe-deposit box at the bank."

"I want to thank you. Just knowing that helped me get through that ordeal."

"I can understand that, JT."

"I know that you stood to earn some extra money for doing that and, well, I wanted to pay you for being someone I could trust. Here is the check we discussed a long time ago when I wrote everything up."

"Aw, JT. I can't take that."

"I want you to have it." He handed it to him, and after a moment's hesitation Jake reached out and took it.

"Thank you, sir." He stuffed it in his shirt pocket, the one with JAKE mechanically embroidered on it.

"As you know, I'm trying to get custody of Corey, and if anyone found out about that letter, it could really blow my chances."

"I see what you're getting at."

"Could you bring it to me, so I can shred it?"

"I'll get right on it."

"Oh, and about the day you went to the baseball game. Who gave you the tickets?"

Jake hesitated. His blue eyes became alert. A flash of a look that meant he'd come to a decision had him answering with conviction. "It was Dr. Berger. He gave 'em to me. Asked me not to say anything."

"Did he come around and talk to you at other times, too?"

"What do you mean?"

"He had a still shot from the video monitor. I was wondering how he got it."

"I…I shut down the surveillance camera when you told me to. I swear."

"As he gave you Dodgers tickets, did he ever offer other things to you?"

"Nah. Uh…once he sent me out to dinner—gave me a gift card, you know? He said I'd been working really hard and deserved a nice dinner out. He said he was going to spend some time with you that night and I looked like I could use a steak."

"When was that, Jake?"

"Uh, I don't remember the exact date."

"Was it on a Tuesday night?"

Jake searched the ceiling for his answer and scratched his head. "Now that you mention it, I do believe it was a Tuesday night. The Dodgers had an away game, and I watched it at the sports bar and steakhouse he sent me to. Yeah, the Dodgers played the Giants that night. It was a Tuesday and they were playing in San Francisco."

"I need to know whose side you're on, Jake."

"Yours, JT! That Berger guy tricked me is all. I should have known better."

He blew out a breath of air and scrubbed his face. "We both should have known better, Jake."

Saturday morning, two months after Morgan had left for college, Mallory made her weekly check-in call.

"Hey, sweetie, I've got a question. Is the university late sending this month's tuition reminders out? I never received a bill."

"Oh, Mom. It's funny you should ask, because I was told it had been paid up for the rest of the semester. They stuck a notice in my campus mailbox."

"By whom? Did they tell you?"

"Well, no. I just assumed you had."

"Could you, please, find out and get back to me? I'd hate it to be some sort of mistake, and then you'd get bounced out of there for having your tuition fee overdue."

"I'll look into it on Monday, OK?"

Mallory hung up and folded her arms. Was it possible she was getting a break? Her? Not likely.

* * *

On Monday evening, Morgan called Mallory around eight, California time.

"It's so weird, Mom. The school said I received a scholarship I don't even remember applying for. Wouldn't you think whoever it was would have sent me an announcement or something?"

"You did apply for a heck of a lot of scholarships. Well, what was it for?"

"Don't laugh. They said it was an anonymous scholarship given for single daughters of single mothers."

"Well, heck, that could go to over half of your class. Not that I'm complaining."

"I know. Well, I'll let you know if I find anything else out."

Something didn't feel right when she hung up. But as this was the best news she'd had in a long time and, Lord knew, she could use more good news these days, Mallory wasn't about to question it. She figured it was about time her luck changed.

CHAPTER SEVEN

THREE months later, JT used every ounce of strength he could muster to push the gym weights away. His legs could hold him for standing and walking but he still needed a walker for balance purposes. The Guillain-Barré had left his nerve conduction lagging behind everything else in his final recovery. His right foot dragged the slightest bit, but it was enough to throw his entire equilibrium off.

No way would he show his face at Mercy Hospital with a walker. Not at forty. Hell, not even at seventy.

He'd worked in conjunction with the other doctors at the hospital to maintain his position as medical director by working diligently at home, much to Wayne Berger's chagrin. He'd conducted meetings via conference calls, had even had a few at his own house. The heads of Medicine, Pulmonary, Cardiology, Orthopedics, and Infectious Disease all reported to him on a regular basis.

And he'd been the main consultant for the ongoing construction of the new rehab wing, which was right on target.

He'd also kept his word to Mallory about conducting a study on Five West for nursing staff needs. He'd managed to approve one extra RN for sixteen hours a week to work every Monday, their busiest day, and every other weekend, thus giving the rotating weekend nurses one more body to add to the mix. He wondered if she had any clue he was behind the study and staffing change.

He itched to be back on the hospital premises—to be part of the routine of medical life again, and most definitely to see Mallory again, if only in a professional capacity. It was better than nothing.

Today, at the end of his feverish workout, the physical therapist grinned and handed him a cane.

"Try this," he said. "It'll give you more balance and loads of character. All you need to do is scowl all the time and the ladies will follow you like rats to poison."

"Are you saying women like to be mistreated?" JT wiped his neck with the white gym towel and thought about a well-known television series where the star was a surly grump with a permanent two-day growth of beard.

He remembered being a grumpy patient a while back, and being forced to shape up by an annoyingly chirpy nurse with the sweetest face he'd ever seen. His scowl hadn't gone over well then, and he'd never dream of mistreating her. Though that's what he'd wound up doing, hadn't he? He'd practically cost Mallory her job. He could only guess how he'd hurt her by dropping out of her life without so much as a phone call. But it had to be, and he'd felt the loss of Mallory with every aching breath since. Surely she'd understand his disappearance had been for her own good.

The therapist prodded him with the cane. "Try it."

His arms were better developed than they'd

ever been. His legs felt stronger, too. If it weren't for his one weak foot, he'd be in prime condition.

He narrowed his eyes, and tried to figure out if his therapist was pulling his leg or was really suggesting he walk with a cane. Slowly, he reached for the institution metal cane.

He stood and used the cane on his right side— it provided just enough added support to help his minor limp. He took a few trial steps. Fantastic! He could walk on his own. Back and forth, back and forth he wore a path across the gym as he practiced moving with his newfound balance.

When he'd exhausted himself, he grinned at the therapist, gave a jaunty hop and tapped the rubber tip of the cane on the floor. "You have anything in black?"

Mallory went down the pre-op checklist for her patient. All was in order. His most recent labs were on the chart, type and cross-match complete. History and physical had been dictated and placed on the front of the chart. And, most importantly, the consent had been signed.

She'd rechecked his large-bore IV to make sure it hadn't clotted off, and after that she'd given him the first sedative an hour before his scheduled surgery time, as ordered.

She removed his wedding band and gave it to his wife, who kissed him on the forehead and said goodbye when the burly transportation orderly arrived with a gurney.

"You're going to be fine, Mr. Roberts," she said in her most reassuring tone, and patted his shoulder. "Once they get that appendix removed, you'll feel like your old self again, shooting under par on the golf course. I'll see you back here in a few hours."

She helped the orderly position Mr. Roberts, who was already succumbing to the power of the shot, onto the gurney and followed him out the door.

As she walked, her mind wandered and she thought about Morgan's upcoming visit during Thanksgiving and got excited thinking how great it would be to see her again. At last someone would be rattling around in her condo besides her. Oh, and Priscilla. Morgan hadn't met the cat she'd gotten from the animal shelter a couple of months ago, when she hadn't been able to bear the empty house another second. Though once she'd gotten to know her cat better, she'd started calling her Prissy instead.

Mallory smiled, thinking about her petite calico cat, and her gaze drifted upward from her clipboard. She almost stumbled when her eyes locked with the unforgettable blue of Dr. J. T. Prescott's. The same mesmerizing eyes that had haunted her dreams and fantasies—blue, rimmed with thick black lashes— stared back. The man who'd hurt her so deeply she'd been unsure if she could ever trust again was writing in a chart at the nurses' station.

He looked up at the exact moment she'd exited the patient's room.

The air blew out of her lungs and her throat went into shutdown mode. Her circulation did an explosive dance around her heart, then vanished and reappeared somewhere by her ankles. She couldn't break away from his stare, though she ached from the rush of emotions. But she'd been deprived of his handsome face for far too long, and as if a moth to a deadly light, she couldn't look away.

His thick black hair had been trimmed to a shaggy style with a hint of natural waves at the neck and above his ears. He was standing! A cane hung freely from his arm while he leaned against the nurses' station counter to write. He looked only at her. His mouth stretched softly into a subtle greeting.

Her hand flew to her stethoscope for something to hold onto. What should she do? Part of her wanted to run up, throw her arms around him, tell him how fantastic he looked and how great it was to see him again. But she'd been kicked out of his life. She'd been banned from being his friend.

Another part of her wanted to scream at him, How could you leave me on my own to be eaten alive by those vultures? But she couldn't let anyone around her have a clue how earth-shattering his appearance on the ward was today.

She gave a quivering smile, her glance flitting away and back, and before her legs could give out she sat down. The emotional wounds she'd so carefully concealed over the last few months had burst open.

He merely looked perplexed over how to handle the greeting. His brows came together with a quizzical stare when she seated herself. She'd almost lost her job because of him, and he'd been fighting for the right to have his son live in his home. Surely those were good enough reasons to part ways. He'd been put on the spot along with her, though she'd never been able to convince herself of that.

Their brief lustful experimentation—and that was all she could sum it up to be as they'd had such little time together—had cost them both dearly. Had it merely been the excitement of taboo sex with a nurse for him? To her, their friendship and physical closeness had meant much more. Did he feel anything at all for her?

Mallory tore her eyes away from him, reached for a chart with a trembling hand and pulled it toward her at the ward clerk's desk. She'd have to do everything in her power to distract herself from him—it was the only way she could survive the moment.

She flipped open the chart with an aggressive clatter. If either was going to approach the other, *he* should come to her.

There'd been nothing tentative about JT's feelings for Mallory. He'd fallen in love with her, pure and simple, and that feeling hadn't changed in the four months since he'd last seen her. Mallory and Corey were the two reasons he'd pushed himself when he'd wanted to curl up and die from the after-effects of GBS pain. Remembering her face had given him strength when he'd struggled to take his first steps. The memory of their passion had driven him to get strong again so he could take her in his arms and be totally in control the first time they made love. He promised himself there would be a first time, and then a thousand times more. Though at this moment, by the look on her face, he wasn't so sure she'd ever give him a chance to make things right.

That morning he'd wanted to clap his hands when he'd learned that one of his patients had been admitted to her ward, and had looked forward to seeing her all the way up in the elevator. Any excuse to see her again would do. Only thinking of himself, he'd been foolish enough to forget the pain he'd caused her.

There she was, looking visibly shaken by him invading her territory. And could he blame her? She'd floated outside the patient's room like an unsuspecting apparition with striking red hair and great legs. He'd been in the desert too long and she was the cool long drink he needed. Yet when she'd looked at him with such confusion, anything but certainty had registered in his mind. His hand gripped the pen too hard when he signed his name in the chart, making it look like a forgery.

Get a hold of yourself.

What could he say to her?

People who didn't give a damn about either of them had kicked Mallory out of his life, and he'd allowed it to happen.

But today was not the time to sort things out between them. Now was the time to re-establish his medical credentials in his regular medical practice, especially since he'd given up the medical directorship. The news would be made public before the end of the week.

Last month, after hearing of Samantha's engagement plans, he'd called Joel Hersh, who'd agreed to run against Wayne Berger for the medical directorship. When the vote had come in from the heads of all of the departments, it had been unanimous. So much for a wedding bonus for Wayne Berger.

Rumor had it that Samantha was now reconsidering their engagement, which meant she'd cling even tighter to Corey. JT's lawyer was the best his family wealth could buy. Though his son was still at stake, and he had to be careful.

JT offered a faint smile for the love of his life. Bear with me, he wanted to say, trust me, things will work out. She didn't return it. Instead, she sat down and grabbed a chart.

Somehow he'd make it up to her. When the time was right, he would find her. They would be together.

Just not yet.

A young nurse stuck her head out of a patient's room. "I need a doctor," she called out. "Stat!"

* * *

Jenny's call for help snapped Mallory out of her state of shock. She jumped to action and ran for the crash cart, just in case a code blue was imminent, and pushed it into the patient's room.

JT was already at the bedside, listening to Jenny's barrage of info and examining the patient.

"The night nurse didn't say anything unusual about this patient," Jenny said. "I came in to do vital signs and discovered he can't talk and his right side is flaccid."

"What's his name? What was he admitted for? What are his vital signs, blood pressure, heart rate, and oxygen sats?"

Using every ounce of control she could muster, Mallory stood quietly at the bedside, waiting for orders, and ready to step in if Jenny panicked. She'd find a way to stop her trembling hands even if it meant sitting on them. She dug them into her smock pockets and watched the doctor she remembered from years before back in action.

"Jorge Torres. He was supposed to have routine gall-bladder surgery two days ago, but they had to open him up when complications developed with the laparoscopic procedure. His last blood pressure was taken at 4 a.m. and was 165 over 98. I was just coming in to do 8 o'clock vital signs. His respirations are regular." She wiped the corner of the patient's mouth then put the blood-pressure cuff in place on his arm. "It's 170 over 102."

Deciding she couldn't just stand around and be useless, Mallory applied the pulse oximeter to the patient's finger and waited for it to register his oxygen level. Keeping busy so as not to watch JT another second, she set up the suction machine on the wall at the head of the bed, and used an oral suction device to remove the excess saliva from the patient's throat.

"Mr. Torres, do you know where you are? Can you shake your head?" The patient gave a lopsided nod. JT examined the head for any recent injury with gentle, caring hands.

"OK, his sats are fair, 94 per cent," Mallory said, removing the small device and stepping out of the way again. If only she could hide in the shadows.

JT took hold of both of the patient's hands.

"Squeeze my hands, Mr. Torres. As hard as you can." The familiar look of genuine concern covered JT's face.

Mallory watched as Mr. Torres gave his best attempt to squeeze back, one hand noticeably weaker than the other.

"That's fine, Mr. Torres," JT said, gently re-placing the patient's hands on the bed.

The patient tried to talk, but it came out all jumbled. His brown eyes took on a look of bewilderment and fear as they scanned the room and watched the strangers around his bed, as if he wasn't sure where he was or what was going on.

"Mr. Torres, I'm Dr. Prescott, an internist. I'm going to check the vessels in your eyes." He removed the ophthalmoscope from the wall and carefully looked deep into one of the patient's eyes, then the other. He removed the stethoscope from his white jacket and listened to the patient's heart for several seconds, then palpated both carotid arteries before listening to them with his stethoscope for any unusual sounds.

Deep in concentration, he moved to the

patient's bilateral pulses, methodically checking his arms at the inside of the elbows, his wrists, both sides of his groin, behind his knees, and finally his ankles and feet.

"We'll need a CT scan stat to rule out infarction," he said without looking up. "Order stat labs, CBC, a chem panel, coags, troponin and cardiac enzymes. Do a twelve-lead EKG. And, Mallory, let's get an IV going. Normal saline. If there's no history of congestive heart failure, run it at 150 ccs an hour. Give him some nitroprusside and titrate his diastolic to less than 90."

Refusing to let her emotions override the patient's priority, Mallory snapped into nurse mode and wrote down his requests, then handed them to Jenny, who ran out the door to process the orders.

Glad to have a reason to leave, she rushed out after her for the IV tray, solution, tubing, and intravenous catheter from the nearby supply cart. Willing herself to keep her mind focused on the patient, not the doctor, she quickly returned.

"We need to rule out everything from hematoma

to neoplasm to ischemic stroke." JT spoke to her like a familiar colleague. Nothing more.

Be still, hands. I've got to get this IV started. Mallory pretended only the patient was in the room, though she felt JT's intense presence as she tied the tourniquet. He had the courtesy to back away and let her work without his scrutiny. Thank heavens, because her hands wouldn't co-operate and she needed to shake them out and regroup before inserting the needle. Once she had the IV in place and running, she walked to the foot of the bed and thumbed through the patient's chart. "It says he's an ex-smoker, he's got high cholesterol and is on blood-pressure meds."

He nodded. JT stood, resting both hands on his cane, watching the patient, deep in thought.

Still jittery, she found the stick-on ECG pads and connected the twelve leads on the patient's chest, arms and legs, then set up the machine to record his heart waves. When she'd finished, she handed JT the results, avoiding his eyes.

"Thank you, Mallory," he said, his voice calm.

She muttered, "You're welcome," and distractedly removed all the sticky patches, coiling the leads and putting them back in place on the portable machine. Anything rather than look at him.

"His heart looks OK. But I want to make sure we don't have any surprise respiratory complications. Mallory, can you open the crash cart? I'm going to intubate him."

She nodded and quickly moved to the large red cart, yanking the plastic lock off with a twist and flipping up the bottom flap before opening the drawers.

"Give me an 8 millimeter endotracheal tube."

She handed him the curved laryngoscope, after checking to make sure the light worked, then a guiding stylet, some lubricant and a syringe, careful not to touch his hands. Where was Jenny? Couldn't she come back and relieve her?

Using his long fingers like the expert he'd always been, JT had the airway in place in seconds.

"Let's give him oxygen through a T-tube."

Mallory found the set-up in the crash cart and applied it, thankful to have tasks to keep her pre-occupied with something other than the man who'd broken her heart right there in the room with her.

"Mr. Torres." JT patted the man's arm and looked him straight in the eyes. He always leveled with patients. "We're going to send you for some tests so we can figure out what happened to you. I suspect you've had a stroke, but we need to make sure with a CT scan. I'll have Nurse Glenn contact your family so they can come in to be with you. We'll do everything we can to resolve the circulation obstruction in your brain. In the meantime, I'm going to move you to the ICU, and if the CT scan rules out hemorrhage, we may put you on some special clot-busters. But I'll let the ICU guy make that decision."

Once the patient had nodded in understanding JT glanced toward Mallory. She quickly flicked her gaze to Mr. Torres.

The laboratory technician arrived, identified the patient and set to work filling vials of blood. She pretended to be fascinated with the procedure, rather than acknowledge JT's lingering presence. No sooner had the lab tech left than the orderly appeared to take the patient for the computerized cranial tomography study.

That left Mallory and JT alone…together, in the hospital room…no longer able to avoid each other. He leaned on his cane and watched her with dark cautious eyes.

Frantic to keep control, and unable to tolerate his stare, she studied the floor, her heart pounding in her chest. She tried to clear her throat, but it had gone bone dry.

He broke the strained silence. "How are Morgan's studies going?"

"Fine." She nodded her head and stared at her clogs.

"Thank you for your help, Mallory."

How could she find her voice to answer? Her eyes fluttered when she tried to look at him.

"Oh, it was nothing. You had everything under control. But you're welcome."

Her attempt at sounding nonchalant fell flat.

"It's good to see you. You look great." Unlike her, he sounded calm, cool, and in control.

It drove her nuts. Here she was feeling as though the world was dropping from beneath her feet, and he was offering casual bedside doctor-nurse banter. Jenny had come back into the room with a large hospital bag, and Mallory had to go along with it. "Uh, um, you do, too." She busied herself by gathering the dirty bedlinen and chanced a glance upward, connecting with his intense eyes again. Adrenaline poured into her system like icy water. Forcing her mind not to go numb, she kept her mouth moving, though she wasn't even sure what she said. "I'm so happy to see you're walking."

"Yeah." He scratched the back of his neck. "Some overly zealous nurse wouldn't let me give up." He leaned both hands on his cane again, and watched as Jenny left the room with the soon-to-be-transferred patient's bag of belongings. "I'll always remember that."

So he did feel something. Maybe not as much as she'd like, but at least it was something. A flicker of hope almost made her smile. She didn't. Did she dare tell him that she'd never forget him either? No. He didn't deserve to hear it.

"Nurse?" A timid voice spoke from behind the

curtain divider. It was Mr. Torres's hospital roommate.

It snapped her back to work. "Yes?"

"I need to use the bedpan."

"Oh." Mallory took one last excuse to glance at JT. She lifted her brows and tilted her head, offering a bitter-sweet smile.

"I guess I'd better go dictate some doctor's notes," he said, resignation in his voice but smiling anyway.

She couldn't resist smiling back, feeling her long-lost connection with JT cautiously coming back to life.

The knock on her door came just before midnight. She was still up, watching the late night shows, as she was unable to sleep, mindlessly petting Prissy who sat on her lap. JT had been on her mind every second since she'd seen him that morning at work.

The pounding frightened her, but the sound was so urgent she couldn't ignore it. From around the corner in the living room she looked down worriedly at her sheer nightgown before asking cautiously, "Who is it?"

"It's JT. Let me in."

Her heart quaked in her chest and left her flailing for composure. She ran her hands through her hair and glanced down at her barely concealed body. Heat rose to her cheeks and melted her center.

"Let me in!"

She walked on wobbly legs the last few steps to the door, unlatched the chain and bolt lock and opened it.

Without being asked, JT blew in like a whirlwind, closing the door behind him before sweeping her off her feet. There was no doubt why he'd come.

His strong arms reached for her waist. He lifted her up and sat her on the nearby small entry table against the wall. His lips claimed hers just as quickly. Instead of thinking how angry she was at him, out of reflex her hands flew to his neck and pulled him closer. It had been too long and she kissed him back, eager to feel his mouth against hers.

His hands moved all over her, skimming, caressing, kneading, pulling her closer and closer still. Each touch ignited a flame beneath her skin.

No time for thoughts or explanations, only desire.

His hot breath covered her ear. "I couldn't stay away another second. I tried. I swear I tried." He kissed the shell of her ear and buried his face in her neck. He easily found her chill spot again at the crux of her shoulder. "God, you feel good."

He kissed her until she couldn't breathe, but she didn't want him to stop. He tasted wild, like pure passion. His hands had easily found their way under her nightgown. Cold from the night air, they found the heat of her breasts and she shuddered. He cupped and lifted her, sending shock waves across her chest. He moaned and covered one of her nipples with his mouth, over the sheer fabric.

She sighed and pushed against him, willing him to pull her nightgown over her head and silently begging him to take off his clothes. As though he'd read her mind, off her nightie came. He shrugged out of his jacket. She pulled at his shirt, desperate to get him out of it. She worked the buckle of his belt and drew him closer once she'd accomplished her task.

The warmth of his torso against hers sent chills fanning out over her body.

She looked into his eyes and saw a fire so out of control it scared her, until she realized he'd come for her, and only she could put it out. She cupped his behind and sucked a flat, tight nipple into her mouth, heard him moan, then felt the strength of his erection between her legs.

She'd dreamed about this moment a thousand times, but nothing came close to this raunchy reality. The smell of male pheromones caused a quickening in her core; she was ready for him.

With her nerve endings flowing like lava, and his firm embrace taking control of her senses, she shimmied toward the edge of the table and opened for him. He lunged with the fury she'd seen in his eyes. With her back to the wall and the wall of his flesh before her, she grabbed onto him for dear life, allowing him to sweep her away to the place deepest inside her. She throbbed and ached with his attention. She gasped and clawed, wrapped her legs around his waist and begged for more. He heaved and pushed and brought her to the brink before she could think one sane thought.

Her first release rolled over her faster than she'd ever dreamed possible. The second built slower and deeper, tensing and straining every muscle she possessed. He thrust at a constant rhythm and she pressed and tightened against his strength. Up and up, soaring above the flesh, she let go with a guttural gasp. He thrust several more times, growled, and quickly followed her lead with nothing less than a primal explosion.

She held on to his shoulders and buried her face in his damp neck and hair, inhaling everything about him. He found her lips again and gave sizzling hot, damp kisses. She returned each and every one, marveling at the taste of salt and satisfaction.

He kissed her forehead, her eyes, her nose. "I've needed you for so long."

She kissed his chin and Adam's apple. "You've got some major explaining to do," she said, breathy and content.

He lifted her and she kept her legs firmly

wrapped about his waist. Still securely connected at their core, he walked.

"So where's your bedroom?"

CHAPTER EIGHT

"Do YOU realize what just happened?" Mallory said from the comfort of her bed, still glowing from their love-making.

"We had great sex?" JT rose up onto his elbow and played with the ends of her hair.

"You carried me from the living room to my bedroom without your cane!"

"So I did." He grinned down at her. "You see? You bring out the best in me."

She cuffed his arm. "Oh, you. It must have been the adrenaline."

"Or the testosterone." He grabbed her wrist and pulled her closer. "Come here. We've got a lot of making up to do. Only this time we're going to take it nice and slow…"

* * *

Just before dawn, Mallory lifted her head from JT's firm, broad chest. She'd drifted off for a brief nap. So had he, after he'd taken her out of the stratosphere and back another time or two with more great sex. My God, the man had stamina. But, like he'd said, they had a lot of making up to do.

Grinning, she pushed her matted hair away from her eyes and studied his face. His angular features were silhouetted by early morning light dappled with the last stealthy patches of night. He looked at peace, a faint smile on his lips. So different from the man she'd first discovered sick and in self-exile. He'd put on more weight and bulked up in his chest and arms from all of his rehab. An indented scar remained where his tracheostomy had been. She couldn't watch him enough after the four months they'd been apart.

And she couldn't ignore the fact that she loved him.

Sensing her shift in position, his warm hand found her shoulder and rubbed it. He turned his head and cracked open his eyes. "Whatever you want, madam. I'm yours for the night." He grinned, waxing dramatic, more sparkle in his gaze.

Mallory stretched with satisfaction.

He hugged her with both arms then flipped her over him and continued rolling until he looked down into her face. "There's something you should know."

She tensed at the words. Their night together had been a supreme fantasy and here came the old "reality" bomb. Mallory braced herself.

"I'm crazy about you," he said.

Her eyes flew wide. She tried not to gasp, but the tiniest catch in her breath escaped.

"You're surprised?" he asked.

"Pretty much. Especially after the way you were so nonchalant at work today."

He kissed her cheek and nibbled her neck while she tried to piece together where and how they fit in each other's life.

"I wasn't sure what you were thinking. A guy needs clues, you know?"

How could she begin to explain the whirlwind of thoughts and emotions that had blown through her mind that morning at work? She'd start with the last day they'd seen each other.

"You let me get fired."

"No, I didn't. There was no winning with Berger that afternoon. I had other plans. I'm sorry if I hurt you, but I had to act like you didn't matter to me." He held her hand and kissed her knuckles. "Please, forgive me."

She inhaled on a quiver. "OK." She'd already forgiven him the minute they'd made love.

He nipped her nose. "Did you know, from the first time I ever saw you I knew you were special."

She sputtered a laugh. "Come on. You never gave me a second glance when we worked in the hospital together all those years. It wasn't until I was the only game in town that you started to notice me."

"I'm a sneaky one. Trust me, you got lots of second glances. But I was a married man. Flirting with the nurses wasn't my style. And I would never categorize you as 'the only game in town.' It would be too hard on my ego."

She knew flirting wouldn't be like him. Still,

it was nice to know she'd at least been on his radar for all the years he'd been at Mercy Hospital. Having gotten to know him better now, she knew he'd have been more direct. If he'd wanted anyone, he'd just have told them. And he'd just told her he was crazy about her!

Dared she tell him how she felt?

JT took each of her wrists in his hands and stretched her arms above her head. He grew intent on his mission and lifted a brow at the sight, nuzzled and sampled the closest breast. She shuddered and grew taut.

"I consider myself extremely lucky." He kissed her neck and shoulder. Chills spread across her chest tightening her breasts more. "Things are different now. I definitely want you in my life."

His mouth covered hers, and she welcomed the warmth and thrill, but knowing they were going to be late if they kept this up she bucked beneath him. He kissed harder, and she bucked again, this time making a noise in her throat.

Finally reading her body language, he lifted his head. "What?"

"We've got to get up and go to work."

He cast a hooded glance at the clock and frowned. "Damn. That does spoil the moment, doesn't it?"

She tapped his rib cage with her finger, gathered the sheet and covered herself to her neck. "You know we should probably set up some ground rules. I mean, for one thing, how are we going to handle this?"

"Daily. With full samples of you." He reached over and swatted her hip then grinned.

"I'm serious."

"So am I." Devilish eyes stared back, and a lock of thick black hair hung over his brow. It took every ounce of willpower she had not to touch him. Looking sinfully great with his one-day growth of beard and blue eyes, he wasn't going to make things easy.

Mallory plopped onto her back and sighed. His hand nestled in her hair.

"Actually, you've brought up a very good point. I'm on the verge of getting full custody of Corey."

She sat bolt upright. "You are?"

"Come back here," he said, gently pulling her by the hair down to the bed.

"That's wonderful news." She smiled and turned onto her side, facing him. Both with bent elbows and resting their heads on their hands— a mirror image—they studied each other.

"I look forward to seeing you like this every morning in my bed," he said, as one hand gently tugged down the sheet, revealing her breasts again. "But we've got to wait a little longer."

Ah, here it comes. She blinked, bit her tongue and, rather than force the subject, thought of something else to say. "How have you gotten Samantha to agree?"

"She's a smart woman. Always has been. She knows it's too hard on a child to be shuffled one week on, one week off between two households. And since my lawyer and Jake helped me expose her underhanded attempts at setting me up and stealing Corey from me while I was ill…well, let's just say she's open to suggestions."

"Oh, my God. That's wonderful."

"As Wayne didn't get the Medical Director position…"

"He didn't?"

"No. Joel Hersh did."

She covered her eyes with both hands and shook her head. "This just keeps getting better and better."

"Tell me about it. So, anyway, I'm taking over half of Joel's patient panel so he can be Medical Director. Combined with my own patients, I'll be a full-time doctor again."

"That's wonderful!"

"Yeah, I'm glad about that, too. And Wayne has applied for a position at Mercy's San Francisco hospital. I'm not sure if Samantha is going with him or not. If she's serious about fighting for Corey, she can't very well plan on pulling him out of school and taking him away from his friends to follow some schmuck to San Francisco. How would that look if I challenged her in court?"

"Have the two of you sat down and discussed all this?"

"Yes. She's on the verge of seeing the light."

With that, the alarm sounded, reminding them they had other responsibilities and needed to get moving.

* * *

Two nurses had called in sick, and as usual Administration couldn't spare another one from any other wards. A tight budget to help fund the new hospital construction for the rehab wing kept Mercy hospital from using a nursing registry. At least, that was what the supervisor had told them.

Mallory, Jenny, and another nurse had to divide eighteen patients between them. The newly hired nurse from JT's nursing staff study agreed at the last minute to work an extra shift when the supervisor had called and pleaded with her. But they'd have to wait a couple hours before she could come in.

Trying desperately to stay on top of things without any sleep, and still reeling from her night of making love with JT, was almost impossible. At 8.30 and already exhausted, she blinked her eyes and trudged on with patient care. Morning vital signs. Patient assessment. Meds for six. Two blood-sugar checks and insulin injections before breakfast got served. Checking all the IVs to make sure they were patent. Three IV piggy-backs to hang before 9 a.m. Help with, or give full bed baths. Send one patient to Radiology for an upper GI series. Draw up a pain shot for another. The list went on and on as she checked her clipboard.

And now Dr. Berger insisted she help him with a bedside procedure on one of his patients. His pursed lips and a disdainful stare made her want to tell him to take a flying jump but she restrained herself from making an emotional outburst.

"Sure. Let me gather the equipment from the supply room. I'll meet you there in a couple of minutes."

And patient call lights never stopped. The ward clerk tried to buzz in to each patient room to find out if it was an emergency or if it could wait. But that was still little help.

Today linen changes would simply have to be postponed until help arrived.

Fortunately, everything she'd need for the thoracentesis procedure was neatly packaged in a sterile tray. The only additional items she needed to find were a couple of large evacuation bottles, in case the patient had a lot of pleural fluid. And as she knew the patient Dr. Berger wanted to tap was a lung-cancer patient, and she'd glanced at the X-rays on the ward's view box, she was certain there would be a lot.

She swept out of the supply room with equipment in hand and two bottles, one under each arm, almost running head on into JT and two other doctors arriving for morning rounds.

One hand in the pocket of his white doctor's jacket, the other gripping the snappy black cane, he wore the same dark slacks he'd burst into her house wearing the night before. Yesterday's shirt had obvious wrinkles from being left in a heap on her floor.

She smiled and could feel the twinkle in her eyes, but he only returned her adoring gaze with a solemn nod and walked on, deep in conversation with his colleagues. The odd interaction jolted her senses, embarrassing her until a blush engulfed her neck and cheeks. They'd just performed every sexual position imaginable, in her limited experience anyway, over the course of several blissful hours. They'd been hot and sticky together, reeking of sex, and all he could do when he saw her at work was nod and walk on? Not even a "Good morning, Mallory?" What the hell was that about? Her embarrassed blush turned to anger.

She'd forgiven him for abandoning her the day she'd gotton fired, and had now been shot down with little more than a glance at work. Who did JT Prescott think he was?

She tossed her head and entered the patient's room, where an impatient Dr. Berger had his patient sitting with forearms leaning on the bedside table.

She bit her tongue and forced down the festering anger, refusing to stoop to strike out at an unlucky substitute.

"Let me get another table to set everything up for you." Bedside procedures could never be completely sterile, but being aseptic was a must. She snatched the tray from the empty patient bed across the room and rolled it over.

Mallory covered the table with blue absorbent towels, washed her hands and donned gloves, trying her best to let go of the hurt and anger JT had just caused. She opened the thoracentesis tray, careful not to touch anything sterile inside the package.

Dr. Berger rolled up his sleeves, palpated and percussed the torso area he planned to tap on his patient, searching for a dull or muffled sound at the site.

"Have you signed the consent, Mr. Owens?" she asked.

The patient nodded his head.

"You'll feel a little prick when Dr. Berger injects some numbing medication, then we'll wait until you won't feel anything but pressure when he inserts the needle between your ribs."

Mr. Owens listened intently. Evidently Dr. Berger hadn't thoroughly explained to him what to expect. "Dr. Berger will only insert the needle into the thin sac that covers your lung. That is where the fluid has built up. He won't be perforating your lung tissue." She glanced up at the doctor with a cautionary look that said, You'd better not. He glared at her with impatient eyes—how dared she take time to explain things to a patient? She ignored him and reached for the oxygen tubing on the wall, reinserting the cannulas inside each nostril of her patient. "Are you allergic to any medication?"

He shook his head. A stoic stare indicated he knew it wouldn't be a picnic, but he was willing to proceed.

Once Dr. Berger had made an "X" where he intended to insert the thoracentesis needle, he opened and put on the sterile gloves from the kit and waited for Mallory to pour germicide into the trough for the cleansing sponge. He grabbed the handle and wiped the skin in concentric circles, tossed away that sponge and used another to repeat the process of cleaning the skin.

Mallory worked diligently, anticipating the doctor's needs by handing him sterile syringes and vials or exchanging smaller needles with larger-bore ones as the topical numbing agent took effect and he needed to go deeper each time he injected.

Dr. Berger tapped into the fluid easily—he was a skilled doctor, she'd give him that, just sorely lacking in a bedside manner and too full of ambition.

Once Mallory had collected a small sample in a specimen jar for the lab, she inserted the tubing into the evacuation bottle, using a stopcock to control the flow. She moved the bottle to the floor, using gravity to help speed up the process.

Fortunately, the fluid she collected looked straw-colored without blood. She hoped it was a good sign for Mr. Owens, but only the lab report would tell for sure.

She patted her patient's hand and smiled. "You're doing great."

He almost smiled back.

While waiting for the rest of the fluid to drain, Dr. Berger got a snooty look on his face and said under his breath, just loud enough for Mallory to hear, "He's way out of your league, you know. He's probably already moved on."

Mallory tried her best not to react to his cruel taunt. The latest report from her bedroom gave any impression but that. Yet he'd managed to plant a seed of insecurity. Especially after what had just happened in the hall. Was she being used by JT? Not about to let Dr. Berger get the best of her, she resorted to undercover—well under bedcovers anyway—tactics.

"Dr. Berger? So sorry to hear about the move to San Francisco," she said with a feigned sugar-sweet voice.

He grunted. Satisfied she'd hit a home run with her sarcasm, she focused back on the job at hand.

Once the procedure had ended, and Mallory had applied a pressure dressing and cleaned up her patient, she helped position him back on the bed so he could rest. With so much fluid removed, he could lie flat and breathe easier. She took his vital signs. His breathing seemed much less labored, and she was satisfied that the 500 ccs of fluid they'd removed had helped him.

She gathered the used equipment and headed for the biohazardous waste container. Her hands were full and her mind was distracted when she caught JT's glance from across the nurses' station. He looked away quicker than she could blink.

Her suppressed anger came to a rolling boil.

After dumping her bundle in the trash, she let

the lid clank shut. She looked over her shoulder and saw JT head for the exit to the stairwell. The rescue nurse had arrived. Mallory whizzed past her and said, "Watch my patients for a sec. OK?"

Without giving the nurse a chance to answer, she rushed toward the exit and pushed through the door. She scurried down the steps to catch up with JT.

"Hey!" she called, not the least bit worried about anyone hearing her. "What on earth was that all about?"

JT stopped and turned with a wide-eyed look. "Mallory, what's wrong?"

"You know what's wrong. You acted like you'd never seen me before in there." She pointed back toward the ward.

He returned up the steps to meet her halfway. "I thought I'd made it pretty clear when I told you about getting custody of Corey."

"What are you talking about? We have to act like strangers?"

"Yes. We'll need to keep things to ourselves for a while longer."

She'd been speeding down a smooth highway

lined with new love and beautiful thoughts until now, when she'd hit a log littering the road to her happiness. "What do you mean? You told me that you were crazy about me."

"Surely you understand. You practically got fired because of me."

"That was when you were my patient. We just became lovers. That's different."

"But it could blow my whole deal with Samantha."

"Why do you give her such power? Your son isn't a bargaining chip. He's a person! She has no right to complain about anything you do on your own time. For goodness' sake, she was dating Wayne and still expected to have Corey."

"Mallory, listen. I can't lose my son. I can't risk it by exposing our relationship. Can't you wait a bit longer?"

"You come to my house, practically break in, take me, and now you don't want to let anyone know? What do you think I am?"

"Hold on. You're mixing everything up."

"No, I'm not. If you were so concerned about appearances, why couldn't you have waited until everything was all settled before you barged into my life again?"

He reached for her hand and kissed her fingers.

"Because I couldn't stay away. I need you too much."

She yanked away her hand. "You sure have a strange way of showing it."

He tried to pull her close again, but she kept backing away, one step at a time.

"Mallory, please."

The insecurity that drove her life flared inside her. She could no longer stand to be near JT. Feeling completely exposed and used, she moved up several more steps. "I've got to get back to work."

"Calm down and come back here." He used his cane to mount the stairs, and grasped her elbow. "Let me explain."

She yanked her arm away and stumbled on a step. He tried to help her, but she backed up another step, and used the wall for balance. She'd willed herself to stay on her feet and pride kept her from falling.

He scratched his head, confusion in his eyes.

He gave her a beseeching look. "What do you want me to do?"

"You told me you were crazy about me. If that's how you feel, don't hide it. I refuse to be your back-street girl. I deserve more than that."

"Mallory, it's just that I can't…"

Tired of spending her life trying to please everyone, living on everyone else's terms, she'd had enough. Finally she would put her foot down, even if it meant risking the best thing to ever enter her life. No. That wasn't true. Morgan was the best thing that had ever happened to her.

JT was just a man. In Mallory's life, men didn't stick around.

Every one of her failures rolled through her mind. She'd gotten pregnant too early in life, and had never demanded that Morgan's father marry her. She'd never even forced him to help support their child. She'd let other men walk out of her life because they didn't want a ready-made family complete with some other man's child. She'd refused welfare, no matter how hard it was to make ends meet. She'd been bullheaded all these years, insisting she could make everyone happy…except herself.

She hadn't asked JT to force his way into her heart. But she deserved to not have to skulk around in the night to be his lover. Now all she wanted was a steady job and a relationship she didn't have to hide. But as that wasn't going to happen, she wanted to be left alone.

"Look, we have nothing else to say to each other." She started back up the stairs.

The door on the floor below opened and footsteps steadily echoed off the walls. The nursing supervisor approached with an interested look in her eyes.

She nodded at JT. "Dr. Prescott."

He nodded back. "Jeanne."

She glanced at Mallory. "Nurse Glenn, on break?"

"I was just going back."

Mallory's eyes skittered away from his earnest stare. She followed the supervisor up the steps and left him on the landing.

"Goodbye," she said over her shoulder.

And a few seconds later, just before she closed

the stairwell door, the lonely sound of footsteps with the added touch of a cane proceeded down the stairs.

CHAPTER NINE

WHAT was he supposed to do now? For a guy who loved control, his life was anything but under his control. He loved Mallory, he had no doubt of this in his mind, yet the timing was horribly off. He wanted Corey to live with him more than life itself, but Samantha still resisted that idea. And until she agreed to the custody swap, he had to be careful. Blast it. He felt stuck.

Yet he could have at least smiled or winked at Mallory at work. She'd made it known how discarded she felt, in no uncertain terms. How could he fix that?

JT returned to his office to calm down and gather his thoughts, but instead, in complete frustration, he banged his cane against the wall. He pounded a fist on his desk and sat. He used the cane to tap on the black cross-training shoes he'd taken to wearing at work for his weak foot—the last reminder of his catastrophic illness—and thought that if it hadn't been for Guillain-Barré syndrome, he'd never have gotten to know Mallory so intimately. He'd never have fallen in love again either.

Ironic. Near death had brought him new life. He scraped his fingers over his jaw. But he'd soundly botched everything up. Was there such a thing as second chances when it came to love?

A knock on his door drew him out of his frustrated thoughts.

"Come."

Expecting his medical assistant, the door opened and Samantha appeared. A chill ran the length of his spine. What now? Her serious expression warned him that he'd yet more drama to deal with on this already emotionally charged day.

"James." She nodded as he stood.

"Is anything wrong with Corey?"

"No. He's fine."

"What do you need?"

"A bit of your time." In another one of her

perfect-fitting suits, this one in some shade of pale green, she sat in the chair opposite his desk and crossed her ankles. "Before I make my final decision to give up custody of Corey, I need to know about this." She removed a piece of paper from her matching purse. "Don't blame Jake," she said as she handed it to him. "I downloaded it from your computer myself. You never changed our password."

He scowled about yet another invasion of his privacy by Samantha, and read the familiar words, starting with "Dear Jake" and ending with explicit instructions on how to shut off power to ensure ventilator failure. His stomach knotted. When he finished reading, he glanced expectantly in her direction.

"You wrote that before you ever became ill. How can I allow Corey to live with someone who doesn't value life?"

"Oh, come on, Sam. You saw what my father went through. He wasn't even able to breathe unaided. I don't ever want to be like that."

"You don't have to remind me about your father. I was there. Remember? Or should I say I was left behind to care for Corey while you were so engrossed with his illness, you forgot we existed."

"Let's not rehash that whole nightmare. Wayne was happily waiting in the wings for you, as I recall. I guess things worked out for the best."

"Perhaps." She raised a brow, a thoughtful flicker in her gaze.

"When I wrote this…" he waved the paper at her "…I had no idea what was coming down the line for me. It was a precaution. Fortunately, Jake never needed to carry it out."

Samantha leaned forward in her chair, engaging his eyes intently. "Exactly. What if the GBS hadn't turned around before your man-made time limit? What if you'd killed yourself, but had you just stuck it out another week your illness would have improved? What about Corey then? Would the rest of your life have been worth giving up rather than spending one more stinking week on a ventilator? One more day beyond what you felt was acceptable in the world according to J. T. Prescott?" She pushed back in the chair and ran her hand through her hair.

"There are some things we just can't control in our lives, James."

Impressed by her impassioned outburst, he admitted she had a valid point. "I *do* know that, Sam. But I'm allowed to state the limits to which I'm willing to suffer, if and when it comes down to a life-threatening illness. It's called an advanced directive. You should have one, too."

"That…" she pointed at the paper "…is called a death wish."

"OK, so it was a bit over the top. I see the error of my ways now."

"Life is sacred. I need to know, for Corey's sake, you'll always want to live. That you won't give up hope too easily."

"I've done anything but given up. I've fought every day to grow stronger. You know I'm a driven man. I don't need a lecture from you." There, he'd done it again, turned Samantha into an adversary.

They sat in silence for a moment. Samantha sat straighter.

"I love him as much as you do, but I know that at a certain age a boy needs his father more than his mother." Her face contorted but she fought off the emotion and forced a smooth visage. "He'll be eleven next month." She tossed her hand through the air. "As crazy as it seems, I love Wayne, but I don't want him to be our son's male role model."

"Well, thank goodness for small favors."

She rolled her eyes. "This is no time for sarcasm, James."

"I know what you're getting at, Sam. Let me add one thing to help you understand. When I wrote this note, I had nothing in particular to live for. You'd left me and taken my son. My father had died a horrible death. I held a desk job I never wanted in the first place. I'd taken it on only to please you. And pleasing you turned out to be impossible."

She started to protest, but he didn't give her a chance. "There was simply no reason left to embrace life and all it offered." He looked soundly into his ex-wife's eyes.

She cleared her throat. "That's all behind us now. I need to know that you don't think that way any more."

It occurred to him that things *had* changed in

his way of looking at life. As messed up as everything had been today with his love life, he felt optimistic for the first time in years.

"I don't."

She tilted her head, sending him a piercing look. "What's changed?"

He sat back in his chair, his eyes drifting upward. What had changed was that he knew without a doubt that he'd want to fight for life, no matter what the circumstances. A lovely redhead came to mind.

"Mallory."

And now that he'd finally realized the extent to which she'd affected him, all he needed to do was figure out a way to get her back.

At four a.m., though it was seven a.m. in Rhode Island, Mallory's phone rang. It was Morgan in her university dorm, up and preparing for class, obviously having forgotten about the three-hour time difference.

"Hello?"

"Mom! I found out some more stuff about that scholarship!"

"What?" Mallory fought foggy thoughts to focus on what her daughter had said.

"Yeah. Between classes, I went back to school administration and found out from a friend of mine that next semester's tuition has been paid, too! She said the scholarships came from the same California citizen as before. That's all they'd tell me. Isn't that torqued?"

"The same anonymous donor?"

"So they say."

Hadn't JT asked how Morgan's studies were going? Why should he care? Well, if he were funding it, he'd certainly want to know. Finally adding everything up, and covering for the fury brewing in her mind, she fudged a congenial response. "Well, let's count our blessings!"

"Yeah, that's what I was thinking, too."

"Do you have any idea what time it is here, Morgie?"

"Oh, shoot! Sorry, Mom. I just wanted to let you know that you don't have to worry about paying anything back."

"OK. I'll see you at Thanksgiving, right?"

"Definitely. I need a break from this campus!"

Mallory hung up the phone and cursed. "Why, that impossible man. Does he think I can be bought?"

Another day on the hospital ward and Mallory's eyes burned from lack of sleep. She hid a cup of coffee at the nurses' station and took a sip before starting patient assessment.

"Can I get a nurse in here?" The familiar baritone voice of JT came booming from Room 5003. She hadn't seen him arrive.

What should she do? Let someone else respond, that's what. She glanced around the ward. Not a soul in sight. She was mad as hell at him, yet they worked at the same hospital so she may as well get used to seeing him.

"You need some help?" she asked, entering the room.

His head sprang up from the patient he tended. Steel-blue eyes found hers and stared for several beats of her heart. His face revealed no emotion other than concern for his patient. Her chest tightened to near strangulation. She attempted to swallow her nervousness and anger, but found her throat uncooperative.

JT went back to auscultating the man's lower abdomen. "Yes. Thank you, Mallory. I've just come from Radiology and Mr. Hartounian needs a nasogastric tube inserted."

She remembered that Mr. Hartounian had had surgery three days before, and had been complaining of increasing abdominal pain. The night nurse said he'd vomited bile early that morning, and portable abdominal X-rays had been ordered.

"A blockage?"

"Yes, paralytic ileus." He glanced at his patient. "Probably due to anesthesia and pain meds."

"Size fourteen French OK?"

He nodded.

If only she could read his mind, what would it tell her? Could he know from the angst in her eyes how she hadn't slept more than an hour or two all night? That she'd tossed and turned and dreamed about being in his arms again? That she'd felt his flesh on hers, and had practically felt him inside her?

That she'd realized he'd paid off her daughter's tuition for the semester, and was as mad as hell?

"I'll order the suction machine while I'm at it," she said, surprised that her voice came out controlled, efficient. Not sounding remotely as intense as she felt. She'd snapped into work mode without realizing it, knowing that while on the job the patient always came first.

Mallory left the room gasping for air. How could she work with him? She wanted to throttle him! But she'd have to toughen up and get used to it if she intended to keep her job.

After dialing central supply for the suction machine, gathering the nasogastric tube and a clamp, some lubricant, an emesis basin and some ice chips, she willed herself to stay calm. Several deep breaths later she returned to Room 5003 where JT remained, chatting with his patient. Any other doctor would have left after giving the order, but not JT. He'd always gone the extra mile for his patients.

With his impeccable bedside manner he explained the entire procedure to Mr. Hartounian, who had been placed in a high sitting position in his hospital bed. When Mallory had put every item on the bedside table, JT glanced up with a diffident smile. Her mouth twitched in response, holding back the furious tirade she wanted to spew at him. She quickly looked away, becoming distracted with setting everything up.

She spread a towel over the man's chest and handed him a cup of ice. "It's really important that you breathe through your mouth or swallow while I insert this tube. OK?"

The patient nodded dutifully, an unsure look in his eyes.

"If at any time you want me to stop for a moment, raise your index finger, OK?" The man nodded again. "And if you want me to stop altogether, you can raise this finger." She tugged on his middle finger, lifted a brow and checked that he'd caught her drift.

Now was no time for sour humor, but Mr. Hartounian smiled for the first time that morning at the chance to give his nurse "the finger." The bit of comic relief helped him relax. And, Lord knew, she needed to, too.

She glanced at JT, who suppressed a naughty

approving smile. A quick flash of him naked and over her with an entirely different expression on his face made her lose control of her hands.

Damn. Get a hold of yourself. Stay focused and angry!

She measured the distance from the patient's earlobe to the bridge of his nose, plus the distance from the bridge of his nose to the bottom of his sternum, using the tube as a measuring tape. She marked it with a piece of tape between the second and third circular markings on the nasogastric tube. Now she knew how far to advance it once inside his nostril and heading toward his stomach.

"OK, Mr. Hartounian, put a few ice chips in your mouth," she said, while liberally lubricating the tube. He did as he was told. "Which side do you breathe best from?" He pointed to the right side of his nose. With expert care Mallory bent the tube and inserted it into his nostril, while he reflexively pulled back. "Bend your head forward, sir."

His eyes grew as round as dark saucers while

she advanced the tube toward the back of his throat. He gagged, and she allowed him to rest and catch his breath.

"OK. Are you ready? Take more ice chips. Now. Swallow. Swallow. Swallow," she repeated, moving quickly before he had a chance to raise a middle finger or to knee her in the ribs. Soon the marking was at the entrance to his nose. "There! I think we're in the right place."

JT placed his stethoscope over the patient's stomach and listened. If the tube was in the patient's stomach, she knew he'd hear a whooshing sound when he injected a few milliliters of air. He nodded at her with a look of success.

For one second Mallory and JT latched onto each other's gaze and held it. Nothing could ever take away what they'd shared in her bedroom. She knew it. From the smoky, hooded look in his eyes, it was apparent that he knew it, too. Heat rose to her cheeks, and she wished she could swallow a few ice chips of her own. If only he knew about the latest information she'd discovered, he'd be trying to hightail it out of the room before she could crown him.

Mallory used hypoallergenic tape to anchor the tube to the patient's nose, careful not to disturb his vision. Shaken by the hot look from JT, she clamped the tube. And with clumsy fingers she attached the end of it to the patient's hospital gown with tape and a safety pin, wishing JT would stop watching her so closely.

"There. We'll hook you up to the suction machine as soon as it arrives."

"You'll get used to the tube, Mr. Hartounian, and it will keep you from having so much stomach distress," JT said, patting the man's arm. "Most likely in a few days the anesthesia-induced blockage will open back up and you'll be back to your old self again. You did outstandingly well."

The patient glanced at Mallory. JT's gaze followed. He nodded. "Yes. She did, too."

Little did either of them know how close she was to decking him. The emotional roller-coaster of having to work side by side with her former patient, ex-lover, and now benefactor was practically unbearable.

She forced a smile for the patient, and avoided

JT's eyes altogether. "I'll check back on you later," she said, before she left the room and headed straight for the nurses' lounge to attempt to recover.

Mallory drove to JT's house straight from work. She pounded on the heavy wooden door, alternating with the brass knocker and doorbell. She heard him abruptly stop playing the piano.

JT answered the door. A pleasantly surprised look crossed his face, until he noticed Mallory glowering at him.

"Are you OK?" he asked, one brow raised.

"No!"

He grabbed hold of her wrists. "What's going on?"

"How dare you?"

He held her at bay. "How dare I what?"

She tried to kick his shins, but he moved out of her way. "Do you think I can be bought?"

"Look," he said, backing her into the wall and pressing his forearms against her shoulders to hold her there. "I don't know what you're talking about."

"You paid Morgan's university tuition, didn't you?" Feeling pinned in, she tossed her head and kicked more. He swung her around and grabbed her by the waist, lifting her feet off the ground and carrying her, kicking and screaming like a kid, to his living room.

"Are you going to calm down?"

"No!" she screamed, fury coursing through her veins, making her heart feel like it might explode. "I'm not for sale. You can't buy me with your guilt money."

He lowered her onto the sofa and covered her with his body.

She wanted to stay angry but, overcome with emotion, tears brimmed in her eyes. She tried to stop the tears by squeezing her eyes tight. Instead, they poured down. Too late, he'd seen them.

He looked at her with a contorted face, raw with emotion. He was hurting and confused too, but she couldn't let him off the hook.

"I never meant to hurt you, Mallory. I just wanted to help you and your daughter. You'd given me so much."

She flailed her arms and kicked her legs,

throwing another tantrum. "You're the one with a guilty conscience, not me. You can't commit, so you tried to pay me off."

He pressed her in place so she couldn't hurt herself, or him. "I wouldn't dream of trying to buy you off. You're priceless."

She thrashed from side to side to keep from looking at him. If he thought she was priceless, he had a lousy way of showing it. She would have called him a liar if his lips hadn't crashed down on hers hard and fast.

She balled her hands and tried to knock him senseless. He dodged her fists with amazing accuracy. His lips held firm to hers.

"Calm down," he repeated over her mouth like a mantra until she quit fighting. "I just wanted to help you." He backed off and held her face with a steely grip, forcing her to look at him. "Don't you see?" he pleaded. "I care about you."

What she saw was desire in his eyes, the last thing she ever wanted to see in him again.

"You should have asked me first."

Deciding the only way she could get free was

to stop resisting, she held perfectly still. The moment he let up, she used all of her might and leverage to flip him over. They tumbled off the sofa and onto the floor. She landed on top of him, feeling his hard ridge where she straddled him. Fury and mindless passion drove her to rip his shirt open. He did the same with the snaps of her uniform then undid the hook on the front of her bra. With her breasts bared, anger pierced her heart, or was it passion? Why couldn't she think straight?

She writhed over him, and her hair fell loose over his chest. She tore at his pants, undoing the zipper and releasing him, hard and throbbing.

Out of control, she tortured him, skimming his taut, throbbing flesh, matching the rhythm of his hips until she was wet and ready. He ripped her flimsy thong free. She rose above him and guided his length inside, then rode him fast and furious, until she found release.

He grabbed her hips and rolled her onto her back, thrusting hard and powerfully into her center, until she came again, and he exploded into a heap on her chest.

She'd only meant to give him a piece of her mind. She wanted to hate him and break things off. Yet here she lay, locked in his hot embrace, feeling his spent passion and craving more.

Refusing to give in to his appeal another second, she pushed him aside, rolled away, and jumped up. Lightning quick, she dressed, minus her underwear, and rushed out of the room, attempting to save face. The shame and disappointment over showing such weakness and losing control threatened to overwhelm her. How had she let this happen? What was it about him that drove her to such mindless things?

I'm a fool for loving a man who doesn't love me. He's thankful to get his life back. That's all.

"I never want to see you again!" she said when she reached the hall.

"The hell you don't!" she heard him yell, just before she slammed the door shut.

The day before Thanksgiving, in a dark and close lawyer's office, Samantha, with tears in her eyes, signed the papers to give full custody of Corey James Prescott to James Theodore

Prescott. The change in custody would take effect after Christmas.

Wayne stood by, quietly supporting her, the most decent thing JT had seen him do in a decade.

JT bit his lip and solemnly signed his own name on the legal document. It had cost him a couple of hundred thousand dollars to convince her to release Corey to his full-time care. He nodded respectfully toward Samantha when he'd finished. Surely it must be the most difficult thing in the world for a mother to give up custody of her child. But he was a benevolent man— Corey would fly up to San Francisco every other weekend, and he could spend a month every summer with his mother. He wouldn't let her memory go dim in his son's life.

"You may have Christmas morning with him. I'll pick him up in the afternoon."

She cried and dabbed a tissue at her mascara-covered lashes. "I expect to have a part of every Christmas with him, James."

"And you shall." He took her hand in his. "Samantha, I want you to know how much I appreciate and respect this decision." He glanced at Wayne, noticing a pained look on his face. "I wish you both the best."

Wayne gave a grim nod.

Resisting an urge to use his cane to help him click his heels together with joy, he shook her lawyer's hand, and then his own lawyer's hand, and left the office.

Whistling, light of foot and tossing his keys in the air, he didn't let his grin loose until he'd reached his car and tapped the horn. He'd celebrate his success by calling his son and telling him he'd be living with him again soon.

No. Samantha should be the first to tell Corey what was going to happen. Better yet, he'd wait and take him to the zoo on Friday, and they'd take some pictures, spend some father-son time, and then he'd break the great news.

But before that he had an errand he needed to run, and it had to do with buying the perfect invitation for the perfect woman.

Having Morgan home for Thanksgiving saved Mallory from spending her extra day off work crying. They danced around the kitchen, Prissy watching with great interest, while they dressed the turkey and prepared the fresh yams.

As they cooked, they caught up on Morgan's dorm life and Mallory's job.

"When's that new hospital wing going to open?" Morgan asked.

Mallory used melted butter to brush over the turkey skin and shook a special mixture of herbs on top of that.

"It won't open until the first of the year, but they'll be having a ribbon-cutting ceremony soon. There's some dedication ball just before Christmas. I don't suppose we peons will get to attend."

"That's harsh, Mom. Nurses keep the hospital going. You should all get to go."

"I don't really care, as long as the powers that be keep signing my paychecks."

After Mallory had enlisted Morgan's help to open the oven so she could put the turkey inside, she sat at the table with Prissy on her lap.

Morgan made herself a cup of instant cocoa and sat across from her. "And what are you going to do about Dr. Prescott?"

Mallory played with the cat's ears, which twitched until Prissy got annoyed and swatted at her.

"I'm going to forget he ever existed."

The brisk, autumn day was perfect for visiting the L.A. zoo. An earlier fine mist had cleansed the air in Griffith Park, and the animals were in great form. JT and Corey had passed the sea lion cliffs, the aviary, even the reptile house, to go straight to the chimpanzees of Mahale Mountains, complete with waterfall.

With the wild and entertaining chimps putting on a terrific show behind the glass cage, Corey giggled.

"How am I supposed to take pictures when they're moving around so fast?"

"Here, let me show you," JT said, taking the camera from his son. He pointed out the lever to adjust. "You increase the shutter time. See?"

The boy screwed up his face, looking unsure.

"As they move fast, your camera has to shoot fast, so you can capture the picture."

"Oh, I get it."

JT smiled at his son, who seemed to be growing taller every day. His thin boyishness was slowly changing to thicker muscles and more adult facial features. He wore an L.A. Zoo ball cap backwards on his head, and a windbreaker with matching shoes that looked more like boats than footwear.

Corey crinkled his eyes to look through the viewer on the camera and snapped several quick shots.

"Wow. This is so cool."

He found a hollow log with a clear plastic barrier somewhere in the middle that allowed him to crawl inside and wait for a chimpanzee to join him on the other.

"Be sure not to use the flash in there. It will scare them," JT said.

"Wow!" Corey exclaimed. "I got a picture of one really close up! I think it was Jake."

JT and Corey had read the names and bios on no less than twenty of the captive chimps on their way into Mahale Mountains. Jake. If Corey wanted to think it, JT wasn't about to burst his bubble. He couldn't tell one chimp from the other.

"Would you like to go with me to Kenya next

year?" he asked Corey when he crawled butt first out of the log. "We can take pictures of all sorts of animals but in their natural habitat."

"Yeah! Can we go see the lions now?"

"Sure."

As they retraced their steps back to the lions' enclosure, JT brought up a subject dear to his heart.

"Corey, did Mom talk to you about coming to live with me?"

"Yeah."

"Are you OK with that?"

He looked up at his father and smiled. "Yeah! I don't want to move to San Francisco, and I don't want to live with Wayne. I want to live with you, Dad."

Fantastic. He wanted to hug Corey, but knew the boy had reached the stage where any public display of affection was off limits. Instead, he offered a high five. "I want you with me, too."

Corey jumped up and hit the palm of his father's hand with confidence.

Across the way, a young woman shared an ice-cream cone with two small children in a double stroller. She had waist-length red hair.

"Look, Dad. She looks like Nurse Think Fast."

Great. Even his son couldn't distract him from his private thoughts about Mallory.

On Friday, Morgan brought in the mail. Her eyes glittering, she waved a bright red envelope. "Look at this. It's addressed to you, and it's handwritten with gold ink."

Mallory narrowed her eyes, suspicious. She snatched the letter from her daughter and sat on the couch. She held it up to the light, but couldn't see through the paper. Morgan sat close beside her, practically breathing down her neck.

"What is it? What is it? I can't wait."

A fine tremor turned to outright shaking when Mallory opened the envelope and realized it was an invitation from JT.

Still angry with him, she hesitated. Morgan tried to take it from her hands, but Mallory waved her off. If anyone was going to open the letter, it would be her.

Dear Mallory,

You are hereby requested to attend Los Angeles Mercy Hospital's dedication ball for the Mercy Revives Rehab Wing—our state-of-the-art, one-hundred-patient bed rehabilitation center on Saturday December 8th.

There will also be a special award given for outstanding care provider of the year, based on ballots cast by patient surveys and general comments from on-the-spot recognition forms.

If this isn't enough reason for you to wear a sexy red dress, you should know I intend to make a special announcement, which I think you will be interested in hearing.

I'll reserve a seat beside me. Be there?

Truly yours, JT.

P.S. Don't make me come after you.

"Oh, my gosh, Mom. That is so romantic."

Not exactly the apology she'd hoped for. The invitation struck her as being as impersonal as their professional relationship. So that's how things would be. Yet he did promise some sort of announcement.

"Big deal, so it's some stupid dedication event.

Who cares?" She did, she knew she did, and worse yet, Morgan knew what a lousy liar she was. "'truly yours'?"

Hmm. She clutched the invitation as though it might disappear.

Was this all she had left of JT? She stood still, holding the invitation, feeling him through the paper. Tingles poured over her as if they were a message. *It's not over yet.*

"Come on." Morgan stood.

"Where're we going?"

"We're going shopping!" She grabbed Mallory's hand and tugged her up.

"But the day after Thanksgiving is known to be the busiest shopping day of the year."

"Too bad." Morgan picked up Mallory's purse and pushed her toward the front door. "He said to wear a red dress, and it's my job to make sure you pick the right one."

CHAPTER TEN

J.T. HAD been ready for hours. He'd slicked back his hair with gel and shaved as close as he could get. Hell, he'd even slapped on some cologne.

He sat in his boxers, shirt, and vest at the piano, so as not to wrinkle his pants or jacket. He'd had his best charcoal colored pinstriped suit cleaned and pressed, and had decided to dress it up with a starched shirt and winter-white wide satin tie.

He needed time to think, and playing the piano always afforded him that. The state of his life came in bits and pieces. Fear drove his life. Fear of winding up like his father had made him a control freak. Yet he'd faced his greatest fear— complete helplessness—and survived. He knew he'd been one of the lucky ones. Now another kind of fear kept him quaking in his dress shoes—loss. He was afraid he'd lost the best chance of his life. Mallory.

He played a Debussy song. Except in his mind's eye the flaxen-haired girl in the song now had gloriously red hair.

Seeing her in the hospital from day to day was almost more than he could take. In a perfect world he'd have told Mr. Hartounian that he was a lucky man to have Mallory, the woman he loved, as his nurse. But, no, he'd swallowed his true feelings and acted the part of physician with nurse. Behind the mask, his emotions dug down to his soul.

As he stroked the keys on his baby grand, he sorted out what he wanted to say later that night and how he intended to say it.

Softly playing the last chord of the piece, he envisioned Mallory's face—wide-set amber eyes and sweet, kissable mouth, and, of course, her hair. With her vision firmly implanted in his mind, he knew what he must do. Finally at peace, he smiled.

Mallory hardly recognized herself standing in front of the mirror. She looked dressed for a prom, except way too sexy. Morgan had insisted on the strapless persimmon-colored cocktail-length dress. Now, pouring over the top of the tight fitting bodice, she wondered how she'd let Morgan talk her into it.

"You don't have to actually *be* huge to look huge, Mom," Morgan had said, before handing her some sort of wonder-producing bra. She stared down her newfound cleavage. Wow.

"Oh, gosh," she whispered, and fluffed her hair. Where was her daughter now, when she needed her for moral support?

Her cellphone rang like magic. Knowing it was her mother's big night, it had to be Morgan.

"How do you look? I can't stand it. Oh, I know, take a picture of yourself with the cellphone and forward it to me."

"How am I supposed to do that?"

"Mom! Do like I always do—hold your phone at arm's length and snap! Then take a picture of the shoes. I've got to see the shoes."

Mallory giggled but did what her daughter had instructed. More tips followed on how to forward the pictures to Morgan's cellphone.

She'd intended to wear her hair up, but Morgan's hairdresser insisted she trim six inches off the bottom and wear her hair down, parted on the side, with lots of thick waves and curls for best effect. She'd wondered if the classic style would last the night. And, worse yet, she worried that her natural hair color clashed with the dress. At least her pedicure and manicure matched perfectly.

Her phone rang again.

"Mom! You look hot! Wow. I knew it was the perfect dress!"

"Oh, sweetie, wish me luck."

"The way I see it, when Dr. Prescott sees you, he won't stand a chance. Trust me, you don't need luck."

"I love you."

"Ditto, Mom. Call me the minute anything great happens, OK?"

"OK."

She hung up and twirled around to check out the back of the dress and hoped she wouldn't fall off the silver high-heeled sandals. The slinky fabric hugged her rear and hips to perfection. Wow. Morgan was right. She did look hot.

"Will JT even recognize me?"

I wonder what his big announcement will be tonight?

He'd mysteriously stayed away from Five West for the last two weeks. She hadn't seen so much as a glimpse of him in the cafeteria or in the halls of Mercy Hospital since she'd received her invitation for the new wing dedication ball.

And it was a good thing, too, because she was still mad at him.

Mallory inhaled a deep breath, gave one last fluff of her new shorter hair and used her overly mascara'd lashes to wink at herself.

"Knock 'em dead!"

Arriving fashionably late, Mallory checked in her jacket before entering the ballroom at the large downtown Los Angeles hotel. The flutters in her stomach came in waves. She clutched her bag and pretended to be perfectly at ease, a tense smile on her face. A few familiar faces from the hospital nodded at her in greeting as they gathered in the antechamber for cocktails.

Perhaps a glass of wine would help settle her

nerves. She headed for the bartender, who'd set up in one of the corners, and on the way over snuck a peek inside the huge ballroom. Her breath caught in her throat.

There stood JT looking handsome and tall, his dark, wavy hair touching the top of the collar on his tailor-fitted suit, one hand casually in his pocket, the other being used in conversation. He stood amidst a small group of men and women who looked to be hospital benefactors. All eyes were on him, and he seemed confident in his role as great communicator.

The last bit of anger she'd managed to hold onto evaporated at the sight of him.

He must have sensed her presence. His head turned…and their eyes met. The jolt of mutual recognition made her knees go weak. She almost lost balance on her near stiletto-height shoes when his face lit up and he gave the most dashing smile she'd ever seen. All she could do was stand and grin back at him, frozen to the spot—the near paralysis was entirely his fault. His blue eyes contrasted with the darkness of the suit, and they crinkled at the edges when he beamed at her. Electrical surges of nerves and tingles almost caused a personal power outage. She couldn't have moved if she'd wanted to.

He immediately excused himself from the group and rushed to her side, his stare decidedly darker and more intense as he approached.

"You look gorgeous, sunshine," he said in a husky voice. "Follow me."

He reached for her hand and set off a small burst of fireworks all the way up her arm. She spun around and followed him without having a choice. They snaked through the crowd until he reached a set of French doors and pushed on through.

The brisk December night prevented anyone else from gathering there. Out of sight from the rest of the party he stopped, grasped her arms and backed her into the cold brick wall, causing her to move closer to him. His mouth covered hers before she had a chance to speak.

Hot. Frantic. His lips caressed hers as though they hadn't seen each other for ever. It felt like for ever to Mallory, anyway. She'd missed him more than she could imagine.

His hands cupped her face so he could alternately kiss her, gaze into her eyes and kiss her again. His tongue danced around hers and she gave in to the taste-of-passion-and-wine kisses. Sweet heaven, she wanted more.

Light-headed with desire, her arms anchored around his neck and she dug her fingers into his thick hair when she kissed him back. She found the warm velvet of his mouth and a pleased sound escaped her throat. Only the tightness of her skirt kept her from wrapping a leg around his hips.

He broke the kiss and found her neck. She gasped for air. His hot breath cascaded over her shoulder and chest. Chills fanned across her breasts and tightened the nipples. Heat and moisture brewed in her core. If he'd wanted to take her right here and now, she'd have let him.

The tinkling of a distant bell grew louder. They noticed it at the same time, pulled apart and glanced at each other with a question in their eyes.

A server dressed in a short white waistcoat stepped out the glass door, rang the bell again and announced, "Dinner is served!"

Mallory sputtered a laugh. JT quickly joined her. He leaned his forehead against hers and looked deeply into her eyes. "We'll pick up where we left off later…after my announcement."

He pulled away and said, "Do you see what you do to me? I promised myself I wouldn't lose control. I swore I'd act like a perfect gentleman. All my best intentions flew out the door the instant I saw you. Did I mention you look gorgeous?"

Mallory beamed, touched her lips to his ear and said, "Once or twice." She inhaled his spicy cologne and promised, regardless of what happened tonight, to never forget his scent.

He reached for the handkerchief in his pocket and wiped at his mouth. He smiled again and winked. "You may want to fix your lipstick." He dabbed at her kiss-swollen lips with the handker-chief.

She arranged her hair over her shoulders. "That was one hell of a greeting, Dr. Prescott," she said breathlessly.

"For you, Nurse Glenn, only the best."

He took her hand in his, this time less urgent, and strolled with her back inside the building.

"The powder room is over there." He pointed in its direction. "I'll save you a seat at the table."

Amazed that she'd made it inside the ladies' room door without her knees buckling, she leaned against the wall to gather her wits. Obviously he had been glad to see me. She smiled at herself in the mirror, and then, to her horror, caught a glimpse at how smeared her lipstick was.

After several minutes of fixing her face and hair, she gathered her ever-increasing confidence and walked through the door to join JT for dinner and, more importantly, to await the big announcement he'd promised.

All through dinner their eyes danced together and away from each other. His knee intentionally rested next to hers. The thrill of knowing they'd touch more later that night kept her excited and engaged in conversation with the other guests throughout dinner.

Joel Hersh sat next to her. A small man, he reminded her of a hummingbird. She smiled at him while thinking about his quick entries to the hospital ward each morning at work, even quicker patient visits, then his eventual flitting out the door in record time. Just like a tiny bird. Even during the dedication dinner, he moved constantly, talking, thinking and adjusting the salt and pepper shakers just so.

His wife, on the other hand, was a picture of stately calm. Her harshly sprayed out-of-date hairdo topped off an expensive periwinkle-colored evening dress with glittering jewels around her neck. By the way Dr. Hersh looked at his wife with adoration in his eyes, Mallory figured they were a good match. And she was incredibly thankful that he'd agreed to take over the job that JT loathed so he could pursue his true calling, bedside medical doctor.

At one point JT reached under the tablecloth and held her hand. The feel of his skin sent shivers up her arm. If only they could be a couple in public like the Hershes. If only she didn't have to play by someone else's rules.

When coffee and dessert were served, a familiar hospital personality took to the stage. Rick Morrell, the charming ER supervisor, had once again agreed to host a Mercy Hospital event. Before Mallory had finished her coffee he'd explained the history of the Mercy Revives Life Rehab Wing. And for an explanation of the fundraising efforts he called on his wife, China, the hospital public relations diva.

The young woman with silky black hair approached the stage with confidence. If she hadn't turned to the side and made her baby mound more obvious in the form-fitting black evening dress, her pregnancy would never have been noticed. She beamed with blooming motherhood and passion for her fundraising role. Mallory knew that she'd once been scared to death about speaking in public, but now handled the job like a seasoned professional.

According to China, they'd managed to raise over $100,000 from the local community to assist with the rehab wing.

The crowd broke into applause at her announcement.

"That sounds like something to celebrate," Rick said. "How about some music?"

Again the room erupted with approval, and loud dancing music poured out over the speakers.

"Shall we?" JT asked with confidence.

In all her fantasies of being with JT, she'd never once dreamed about dancing with him. Now was a chance in a lifetime, and she had no intention of missing it.

A crooning sexy song brought Mallory and JT together on the dance floor. He took the lead without a moment's hesitation, one palm firmly planted on the small of her back, the other lifting her hand in the air. He moved gracefully for a big man who until recently had walked with a cane. She hadn't danced in years, but JT was so sure of himself she followed easily.

They grinned at each other and finally she relaxed. JT pulled her closer to his chest and looked into her eyes. The familiar sizzling hooded look reappeared, zinging her with desire. He glanced obviously down her cleavage. "Nice. Remember when I kissed you there?" The hand holding hers for dancing squeezed tighter.

Her eyes widened with an explosion of memories, and she felt heat between her thighs.

He lifted her hair from her shoulder and lightly blew across her skin. "Remember when I kissed you there?" He delved deeply into her eyes with a smoky blue stare.

A jolt of sensations coursed down her spine, she throbbed between her legs with wanting him so much, and didn't think she could bear another moment of his public seduction.

He kissed her cheek. "And here," he whispered into her ear. "I liked to kiss you here."

His hot breath melted the last of her resolve. Why couldn't they just leave, go to her house and rip each other's clothes off? The only antidote for the heat he'd started percolating throughout her body would be the cool flesh of the long and lean J. T. Prescott.

Fortunately the song ended before her breathing became ragged to the point of hyperventilation. The last thing Mallory needed was to pass out in front of everyone from Mercy Hospital and make a fool of herself once again.

Her feelings were mixed between relief that it was over and wishing they could dance longer, titillating and taunting each other with secret glances filled with promises. The other dancers applauded while they all slowly ambled back to their seats.

Mallory lifted a glass of ice water and held it to her cheek. JT gave a naughty half-smile, knowing he was responsible for her flush. She had to look away.

Once the room settled down, Rick invited JT to join him at the podium.

With cool aplomb JT rose, glanced at Mallory with a reassuring wink, straightened his tie and jacket and approached the stage.

Was he ever out of control? Well, yes. When he'd practically made love to her the moment he'd seen her tonight.

She smiled, realizing that she had caused the old control freak JT to lose his composure… again.

When he reached the dais he cleared his throat.

"The only way Joel Hersh would agree to become Medical Director was if I promised to do all of the speaking gigs for him."

The crowd chuckled, especially Joel, sitting to her left, and JT smiled until they grew quiet.

"But, seriously, we come here tonight to celebrate a new beginning for Los Angeles Mercy Hospital. My duty tonight is twofold, to celebrate the opening of our new rehab wing, and to honor the caregiver of the year.

"First, our rehab wing. We live in a time when more and more heroic surgical repairs are being performed, but who takes over when it's time to learn to walk again? Or when a person needs to relearn the activities of daily living after a stroke? How does a patient learn to use that hand we've reconstructed for them?

"In the past, we've always sent our patients to other rehab facilities. But even in a time of the California statewide budget crunch such as we're currently in, Mercy Hospital has been committed to being self-sufficient. After a great deal of planning, we developed the idea to design and build a state-of-the-art rehabilitation center of our own. And thanks to the tireless fundraising efforts of China Morrell and our responsive community, we are proud of our results."

Applause erupted in the room.

"So tonight we celebrate our success and look forward to the dawn of a new day at Los Angeles Mercy Hospital."

A screen dropped down, and music played over a short film made to promote the new facility.

The crowd sat enthralled by their joint accomplishments. When the film ended and the applause died out, JT continued his portion of the evening's presentations.

"Most of you know that recently I was stricken with Guillain-Barré syndrome. I'd never been on the receiving end of medicine until I was sick and helpless. Those who know me well also know I like to be in control of things."

Knowing laughter erupted throughout the crowd. He waited for it to quiet down.

"Yeah, yeah, I know, I'm a control freak. But I had time to think while being held captive in my paralyzed body. I'd been relegated to coexist with my greatest fear—helplessness. During that time I realized how important good bedside care is for any recovering patient. I also learned that there are good doctors and nurses, some not so good caregivers and occasionally, if you're lucky, there are angels. I was lucky. I discovered an angel during my rehab."

He glanced at Mallory. Heat warmed her cheeks. So this was why she was there. He wanted to thank her publicly for being his nurse. A wave of disappointment threatened to bring her down from her euphoria.

"The second part of my task tonight is to announce our caregiver of the year award. This award is given to the nurse or doctor most highly respected by their patients and defined through hospital surveys. You've all seen those papers mailed to your home shortly after your most recent medical encounter. Well, guess what? Some people actually fill them out. And as is often the case, a pattern was noticed with those surveys.

"Tonight it gives me great pleasure to announce the first annual Mercy Hospital Inspirational Caregiver award. The person chosen for this award comes with the seal of approval from the people who count the most in this profession, the people with the most experience. You guessed it, the patients."

Applause broke out for the people who kept the hospital in business—the clients of Mercy hospital.

JT grinned as widely as a Cheshire cat, and Mallory felt he'd been acting as sneakily as one all evening. Why had he dragged her here just for some dumb patient survey award?

"This award goes to my personal angel. The person who assured me that I was in good hands, when she cared for me. The nurse who handled my ailing body with an angel's healing touch. The nurse who willed me to live. So I did."

He smiled gently in her direction. Even Joel Hersh glanced her way.

So this was all it was—an award for being a good nurse. She'd been foolish enough to hope for more. Was she really not worth falling in love with?

"Mallory Glenn, will you, please, join me on stage?"

How could she refuse? The entire audience sat expectantly, waiting for her to stand up. Always willing to please, never wanting to let anyone down, she did as she was told. The cold fingers of disappointment crawled up her spine and pushed her toward the stage.

When she reached JT, he offered his hand, an

anchor she needed to latch onto to keep from falling off her high heels.

He drew her close to the podium and casually let his arm come to rest on her shoulders.

"Doesn't she look beautiful tonight?"

The crowd responded with applause.

Flames lit her cheeks. *Keep smiling. Just keep smiling. Don't let anyone know how disappointed you are.*

"First off, I have a check made out to you, Mallory, for five thousand dollars." He handed it over. She took it with shaking hands.

"That should help with some of Morgan's tuition next year. Oh, and a plaque. Of course a plaque." He handed it to her. She dutifully took it and showed it to the crowd, as if they could read it from a distance.

The crowd chuckled at the absurd requisite gift that seemed to accompany any achievement at hospital awards events.

"But there is a string attached to this award, Mallory. I have a special request."

What was this?

"I observed at first hand your skill and talent

with rehab medicine. I have encouraged Mercy Hospital to offer you the job of Nursing Supervisor of the rehab wing. Will you accept?"

Both angry and shocked by being put on the spot with his invitation, a million thoughts ran through her head. More pay, more responsibilities, more pay, more headaches, more pay, more prestige, more pay. Apparently JT couldn't offer her a personal commitment, but at least he'd made sure she'd be financially set. Though feeling more like it was the booby prize than a golden chance, Mallory was wise enough to recognize opportunity when it knocked. She made a snap decision.

"I'd love to take the job. Thank you." She'd been acutely aware of the need to look out for herself all her life. And as she wouldn't be having a future with JT, it was even more important to take whatever opportunity she'd been offered.

She and JT blandly smiled and posed for a picture together, holding the plaque between them.

"I have one more request," he said with a

sparkle in his eyes. He took the plaque and placed it on the podium.

What else could he want? How else had he thought to torment her with expectation, only to let her down?

"As proof of how great Mallory's rehab efforts have been on my behalf, I'd like to remind everyone that I am no longer using a cane. And this leg…" he lifted and bent his right leg "…now has the ability for full range of motion. Allow me to demonstrate."

He dropped to one bended knee to prove his point. "Mallory, can you help me here, please?"

He reached for the hand she offered and held it, then fished inside his pocket with the other.

Tender eyes stared up at her. He cleared his throat.

"Mallory Glenn, in front of all these good people, and with a promise never to hide my feelings for you again, I'd like to ask one question."

He produced a ring while she fought to keep from falling off her heels.

"Will you marry me?"

Had she heard correctly? J. T. Prescott, the

king of control, had just asked her to marry him in front of several hundred people without having a clue what her answer would be.

Her pulse rate soared. Fireworks went off in her chest. She gasped for breath so she could answer him. How hard was it to say yes?

He smiled expectantly up at her, his hand steady and strong. He held a simple diamond ring in readiness. But she couldn't make herself answer. Sure, she was still angry with him for paying Morgan's tuition fees without asking her first, but wasn't he everything she'd ever wanted? Hadn't he come out of the closet with their romance? My God, the man was on his knees in front of a room full of people!

All she'd ever wanted had been a simple declaration of love, not going overboard like this.

Mallory glanced down at JT, the sparkle in his eyes beginning to wane. A few nervous coughs could be heard in the quiet audience.

This was it, her chance for happiness with a man she respected and loved. Yet she couldn't find her voice.

She'd spent too much time weighing her good

fortune in her mind without giving her answer, she knew it, but this was her life. No longer worried about making everyone else happy first, she ran a brief future of what life with JT would be like through her mind. Awkwardness settled across the crowd. JT stirred, as if he intended to stand up again.

"No!" she shouted.

Disappointment covered his face.

"I mean, stand up," she said. "Please." She shook her hands out, trying to gather her composure. "I want to answer you." She helped pull him up and held tightly onto his hands. "Give me a second, please."

Standing before her, a calm smile on his face replacing the doubt. Deep grooves outlined his wonderful grin. His eyes shone brightly with love and vulnerability. She spent a second taking it all in, wanting to hold that vision in her mind's eye for ever.

"You've said some pretty great things about me, and I think I should let them…" she tossed her head in the direction of the ballroom "…know how wonderful *you* are."

She smiled through blurred vision.

"You are the most courageous man I've ever met, and this crazy idea of a proposal is just another example of how daring you are. The whole time you were sick you blamed no one for your illness. As frightening as everything must have been, you didn't really quit, you just withdrew deep inside to wait for the worst to pass. I realized early on how special you were. You're a survivor. Even sick, you gave me happiness I hadn't experienced in years. And then I made the best discovery I could ever imagine. I couldn't tell anyone how I felt before tonight at the risk of losing my job."

She looked out over the audience, wondering if the powers that be got her message.

"I love you, J. T. Prescott, and my answer to your question now and for ever shall be yes!"

He slipped the ring onto her finger. It was too large so he slipped it onto her middle finger. He shrugged for the audience. She laughed along with them. Life wasn't perfect, but things were definitely looking up.

"I'll get that fixed next week," he said.

Next week. Yeah, they had a future together—next week, next year, ten years down the road.

They stood together and he dug his fingers into her hair to draw her near. They kissed and wrapped each other in a tight embrace.

Applause erupted from the crowd, reminding them they weren't alone. In typical Shakespearian fashion, JT raised a hand and bowed. Giggling like a child, Mallory curtsied, tears rolling down her cheeks. She didn't care that the most intimate moment of her life had been shared with over two hundred strangers.

Rick stepped up to the microphone. "I think we've got something else to celebrate tonight." He cued the disc jockey, who blasted a fun, triumphant dance song.

JT took Mallory's hand and led her out to the dance floor. An unmistakable look of adoration, love, and desire glowed in his eyes. He twirled her around and wrapped her in his arms. Her head rested on his shoulder. He kissed her ear and said, "I want you, Mallory Glenn, for the rest of my life."

He twirled her so she faced him. She beamed

with the rich feelings coming to life inside her. She'd thought she'd known how love felt before tonight. But right now, with the special man in her life staring down at her, she realized that until that moment her thoughts about love had only been a dream.

J. T. Prescott was unquestionably real, and most definitely belonged to her.

And, oh, she owed her daughter a cell phone call.

MEDICAL™

Large Print

Titles for the next six months…

January

SINGLE DAD, OUTBACK WIFE	Amy Andrews
A WEDDING IN THE VILLAGE	Abigail Gordon
IN HIS ANGEL'S ARMS	Lynne Marshall
THE FRENCH DOCTOR'S MIDWIFE BRIDE	Fiona Lowe
A FATHER FOR HER SON	Rebecca Lang
THE SURGEON'S MARRIAGE PROPOSAL	Molly Evans

February

THE ITALIAN GP'S BRIDE	Kate Hardy
THE CONSULTANT'S ITALIAN KNIGHT	Maggie Kingsley
HER MAN OF HONOUR	Melanie Milburne
ONE SPECIAL NIGHT…	Margaret McDonagh
THE DOCTOR'S PREGNANCY SECRET	Leah Martyn
BRIDE FOR A SINGLE DAD	Laura Iding

March

THE SINGLE DAD'S MARRIAGE WISH	Carol Marinelli
THE PLAYBOY DOCTOR'S PROPOSAL	Alison Roberts
THE CONSULTANT'S SURPRISE CHILD	Joanna Neil
DR FERRERO'S BABY SECRET	Jennifer Taylor
THEIR VERY SPECIAL CHILD	Dianne Drake
THE SURGEON'S RUNAWAY BRIDE	Olivia Gates

MILLS & BOON®

Pure reading pleasure

1207 LP 2P P1 Medical

MEDICAL™

Large Print

April

THE ITALIAN COUNT'S BABY	Amy Andrews
THE NURSE HE'S BEEN WAITING FOR	Meredith Webber
HIS LONG-AWAITED BRIDE	Jessica Matthews
A WOMAN TO BELONG TO	Fiona Lowe
WEDDING AT PELICAN BEACH	Emily Forbes
DR CAMPBELL'S SECRET SON	Anne Fraser

May

THE MAGIC OF CHRISTMAS	Sarah Morgan
THEIR LOST-AND-FOUND FAMILY	Marion Lennox
CHRISTMAS BRIDE-TO-BE	Alison Roberts
HIS CHRISTMAS PROPOSAL	Lucy Clark
BABY: FOUND AT CHRISTMAS	Laura Iding
THE DOCTOR'S PREGNANCY BOMBSHELL	Janice Lynn

June

CHRISTMAS EVE BABY	Caroline Anderson
LONG-LOST SON: BRAND-NEW FAMILY	Lilian Darcy
THEIR LITTLE CHRISTMAS MIRACLE	Jennifer Taylor
TWINS FOR A CHRISTMAS BRIDE	Josie Metcalfe
THE DOCTOR'S VERY SPECIAL CHRISTMAS	Kate Hardy
A PREGNANT NURSE'S CHRISTMAS WISH	Meredith Webber

◎™ MILLS & BOON®
Pure reading pleasure

1207 LP 2P P2 Medical